A CHANCE TO
LIE

A CHANCE TO LIE

By Shadé Akande

Universal Etch Publishing
130 Seventh Avenue, suite 127
New York, NY 10011

Universal Etch Publishing Subsidiary Rights Department

130 Seventh Avenue, suite 127, New York, NY 10011.

First Universal Etch Publishing hardcover edition April 2014

For information about special discounts for bulk purchases, please
contact Universal Etch Publishing Special Sales at
sales@universaletch.com.

Jacket Design by IJ Creatives

Manufactured in the United States of America

1   3   5   7   9   10   8   6   4   2

Library of Congress Control Number

Akande, Shade

A Chance to Lie : a novel / Shade Akande.

2014936496

ISBN 978-0-9960-6241-1

ISBN 978-0-9960-6240-4 (ebook)

To You, reader.

I've been looking forward to this day. Enjoy!

THE (FIRST) LIE

I coughed and woke up in a hospital bed surrounded by members of my family. When I opened my eyes, they were all staring at me, and it seemed as if they were holding their breaths. I didn't say a word. I wanted someone to say something, so I'd know what was going on because something was definitely going on.

The doctor entered the room, and the quiet was loud. She walked to the head of my bed and asked me if I knew where I was, and I nodded. The metal bed, her stethoscope and non-flat-screen television on the wall told me that much. Then I looked around the room. My parents were there. They looked as though they'd been crying for days. My Aunt Janet was wearing her favorite green dress. *She has such great style.* And she was wearing that "natural" deodorant again. I could smell her from across the room. *Gosh. Maybe that's why my parents are crying.* I also saw my brother, and, on my right, almost on his knees, my husband was leaning on the side of my bed. In the far-right corner of the room was my best friend, Elly. She looked distraught.

The doctor asked me if I recognized anyone in the room. I shook my head. My mom began to cry, and my dad consoled her. My husband dropped his head in his hands, and there were some other movements and sounds in the room. It was weird, but I felt relieved. I could still smell my aunt, though.

I wasn't sure what had happened to me. I looked under my covers to check my legs. They were both there, but I was sore. I looked at my reflection on the metal bars of my bed and saw a couple of minor bruises on my face, but they appeared to be healing. I tried to ask, "What happened to me?" but I just ended up coughing and clearing my throat. The doctor put a stethoscope to my chest and said, "It's okay. Just relax." She asked everyone to leave the room, and then she waved in a few more doctors. My husband touched my hand then kissed my forehead before leaving. I took a deep breath and wished I could be a fly on the other side of the wall to listen in on my family.

When the doctors left me to sleep, I had a dream that resembled my life so much I thought it was real. In the dream, my family members were in a hospital room, and I had an aerial view of everything. It was almost as if I was dead or about to be, because I could also see myself motionless in the bed. My mother was talking to my husband, Eric, and she asked him what he was going to wear to an upcoming awards dinner. *Really, mother? I'm laid out in the hospital, apparently broken or something, and that's what you discuss?* Eric mentioned a couple of designer suits, not because he cared much about fashion but he loved the attention that my mother gave him and knew it would also impress my *fashionista* aunt. And, clearly, he didn't consider this inappropriate deathbed conversation, either. Eric then began to explain which award he was receiving and why he was receiving it ... again. He tried to sound modest, but Dad's expression suggested that once again Eric's attempt at *modesty* was unsuccessful. *Oh, Eric ...* I love him regardless and, well, Eric loves Eric too. Dad walked away from that conversation to put headphones on me, knowing how much I loved music, and hoped it would help somehow, and then he paced the room.

"Eric, have you eaten anything today?" Mom asked.

"No, I don't want to leave the room. When she comes to, I want to be here."

That's the part of him that I do love, and it made me smile until Mom said, "She's so lucky to have you."

That was her line. Since the day I got married, almost ten years ago, my mother hadn't let a moment pass without telling me how lucky I was to have Eric. At first, I loved hearing that, but after about year one, I learned that what Mom really meant was that without Eric, I wasn't much. I've since loathed hearing how *lucky* I am, and I would say something to her, if I didn't partly believe it myself. I mean Eric is a successful, accomplished, and attractive man, definitely a catch.

Growing up, my academic achievements weren't really acknowledged by Mom, but whenever I got dolled up, she made a big deal out of it so, by high school, I focused more of my time on my looks and fashion. My perception of things and ambition really changed during that time. I went to college but knew that all I had to do was show up to get what

I wanted—so long as I showed up pretty. And being attractive got me far, but even *far* had its endpoint. I went from being smart, to being the center of attention, to being the wife of a *smart center of attention*. If I could do it all over ... I had a decent career now, but it came nowhere close to Eric's success or, more importantly, the success that I shorted myself. Anyway, back to my dream ...

My mother tried to persuade Eric to grab a bite, but he assured her he was all right. Then she offered to get some food for him. My sisters entered the hospital room, which should have been an immediate indicator that this was a dream, not because they both comfortably and inappropriately took seats on my bed—moving the feet of my comatose body for more room—but because both of my sisters detested me, so visiting me was quite the stretch. Growing up, we were really close, and they looked after me, being my big sisters. But when each of them got divorced and then I got married, things changed. Now they hardly spoke to me at all.

"How long are you guys staying here?" asked my sister, Lisa.

"I'm not leaving," Eric replied.

"I was talking to my parents."

"Lisa, be nice. Your dad and I are staying here with Eric." *Wow.* Not staying with *your daughter?*

"I feel like Bailey is going to come to today so we should be here," said Dad. *My dad is the best.* "Where did you two run off to anyway?"

"We've been in the cafeteria," said Lisa.

"Yeah, and the food is nasty," said my sister Tina.

"It's not that bad," said Lisa.

"You didn't think to bring any food for us?" asked my Aunt Janet.

"I did. I sent Mom a text, but she didn't reply," said Lisa.

"My phone is off. You can't have your phone on up here."

"Oh, then we need to go, Lisa. I'm expecting a call, so I can't have my phone off," said Tina, now standing.

"You're going to leave? You two didn't even spend any time with your sister. Isn't now the time to put all your differences aside?" Dad asked.

Lisa walked up to the head of my bed with arms crossed and said, "If she wakes up, I can put my issues aside."

What? Hearing that, I coughed and then saw myself in the bed coughing. Then everyone looked at each other in shock, and I thought it would be reconciliation time. But then I woke up and realized it was only a dream and I was alone in a real hospital room.

THE RELEASE

I stayed in the hospital for a few more days and, during that time, I learned that a car accident put me there. A large vehicle hit the passenger side, and I had been in the passenger seat. I asked if anyone else was injured or killed, and my doctor said no. *Thank God.* When I asked who was driving the car, she said my family should give me those details. *Okay …*

After the ambulance got me to the hospital, I fell into a coma for about a week and, although my injuries didn't appear that severe on the surface, the doctor was unsure of what the outcome would be. There was some head trauma, so the doctor warned my family of a slight chance that I'd suffer retrograde amnesia when I woke up, which is a loss of access to memory of events or information that occurred before an injury.

My arm moved a little, the first of any movement in seven days, so my family rejoined Eric at the hospital. When I woke up from the coma several hours later, everyone was glad but on edge, wondering if I'd remember any of them — remember anything really. So, when the doctor asked if I recognized anyone in the room, and I shook my head, their fear that I'd have amnesia became a reality — except for the fact that I didn't actually have amnesia. I did have more gas than usual, though.

I could've just told the truth, but everyone was actually concerned about me for once. I pictured my mother turning around to chat with Eric about suits, my sisters continuing their *anti-me* crusade and everything going back to normal with me in the background. I didn't want that to happen because right now everyone was interested in me, and they were actually paying attention to me. Honestly, I didn't know what I'd gotten myself into, but so far, I liked it and hoped I could pull this off ... *faux-nesia* that is.

During my hospital stay, family members visited me with photos on hand and "Hello. My name is" stickers on their chests in aggressive attempts to restore my memory. This sucked because I had looked forward to the fun of messing with them all and maximizing my faux-nesia. What didn't suck was that most of them came bearing gifts. *Yay!* I had to remember not to get too excited when I got gift cards to my favorite stores, which is any store on Fifth Avenue. But even I couldn't fake appreciation when I opened Aunt Cecilia's gift, which was shoes, likely purchased from a place that also sells computers and turkey bacon.

My mother came to visit me yesterday without my dad or Eric, which surprised me. I expected her to come with one of them or not come but have one of them give her an update. She had a couple of bags with her, and I was curious to see what was in them. She took off her goose-down coat, then her cardigan, wool scarf, hat, and then another cardigan from her small frame. She always overdressed in the winter and had done the same to us when we were little. She adjusted her soft salt-and-pepper curls and cleaned her glasses with her sweater — the other one that she was wearing.

"Are you feeling any better today?" she asked.

"Much better. My legs aren't sore, but I still have head pains."

"They've given you something for that, right?"

"Yes, they have."

This weird small talk was less due to my faking amnesia and more of what a conversation with her would be like anyway — if the two of us were ever left in a room together. Once I traded in *books* for *looks*, I was the center of her world for years. Then, when I got married, she shifted her focus to Eric. I'd been trying to win back her attention ever since, so I didn't know what to say to her anymore.

"I have a treat for you," she said then reached into a bag. She handed me a warm Tupperware container. "Macaroni and cheese. It's always been your favorite."

Are you kidding me right now? My mother hasn't done something just for me since forever. I stared at the container in my lap and didn't know if I could respond without getting emotional.

"Thank you. It's my favorite, huh?"

"Yeah, I think it still is. I used to make it for you all the time when you were younger." Then she moved my hair out of my face as if she were reminiscing. She was thinking about something. The combination of mac and cheese and unfamiliar caresses from my mother were about to bring me to tears, but I held them back.

The last time my mother and I exchanged food was a few months ago. I'd come home after work and prepared a great dinner for Eric after confirming with him earlier that he'd be home on time. It was a rainy day; I was bloated, work was stressful, and I had to stop by the supermarket, but I was determined to make a great meal for my husband. Work had been keeping him busy, so we hadn't been spending any quality time together. By eight o'clock, dinner was on the table, but there was still no Eric. I called him. He said he wouldn't be home before midnight. I was livid, but I didn't say anything. I never did.

I called Dad to vent, but he wasn't home, so I ended up venting to Mom. *Mistake.* She didn't understand why I was upset. Eric was working hard *for me* and making a meal that he could eat later shouldn't be a big deal. *Thanks, Mother.* When I was about to hang up, she said I might as well bring her some of the dinner, since she didn't get a chance to cook, with her knees bothering her and all. Ten minutes later, I was in a cab to Brooklyn with a Tupperware container in my lap and mad at myself.

"It's delicious. What else do you have there?" I asked.

"Oh. I brought you some socks and a sweatshirt since it gets chilly in here," she said and placed them on my bed.

Come on now — who is this woman? I was waiting for her to say, "Your dad sent this over" or "Your dad is parking, and he'll be right up" but she never did. It was all her.

"You brought these for me?"

"Of course. I wanted to bring you a space heater, but they didn't allow those when I was a nurse, so I figured I shouldn't," she said. "I'm so glad you're okay, Bailey."

I don't know if it was the meds, but I think I saw my mother tear up. And at that moment, my only *faux-nesia* remorse was that I hadn't thought of it sooner.

The day of my release, my best friend, Elly, came by to see me. I hadn't seen her since the day I woke from the coma. Elly had that girl-next-door beauty, but being smart was really her forte. She was the valedictorian of our middle school and high school classes and was hands-down the smartest woman I knew today. Being an only child, she was also spoiled terribly, but now in her thirties, she'd taken on the responsibility of spoiling herself.

"How are you feeling?" she asked.

"A little tired but okay. I feel like I'm moving in slow motion."

"That's to be expected. I'm just glad that you made it." And then she just started crying. I patted her back until she got it all out, then I handed her some tissue.

"I'm Elly, by the way. I didn't get a chance to mention that the other day. And you and I have been best friends since junior high school." *That's what we called middle school in New York City.*

"We must be," was all that I could think to say. "Tell me about my life in a nutshell, Elly." I thought it would be interesting to hear how she described it. I was the ultimate people-pleaser, especially when it came to my family, even if they were the source of my discontent.

"Well, you're married. You work in marketing at a global beverage company, called knirD woN. You have five siblings and your parents are also in New York. Oh, you live in New York City."

"I knew the New York City part."

"You remembered that?" she asked excitedly.

"Well, no. I've been reading the paper and watching television for the last couple of days."

"Right, of course. Um, what else? You don't have any children yet. Your life is ... good. And you're the best friend anyone could ever ask for." And then she started crying again. I patted her back until she stopped crying and passed her another tissue. *She didn't actually have any tears this time, though. Drama.*

"Okay, this is the last piece of tissue in this room, so if you cry again we're going to have to recycle the *good* corners of some of those un-new tissues in the trash bin."

She chuckled and said, "And you always make me laugh." Her cell phone rang. "Oh, sorry, I forgot to turn this off," she said, looking at the phone. "Actually, I have to take this." She went out to the hall, and closed the door behind her.

She returned a few minutes later, and I said, "So tell me about this husband of mine."

"Um, sure. What would you like to know?"

"Anything. I haven't been able to ask him much yet because other people were always here. Where did I meet him?"

"You met Eric your junior year of college and dated shortly after. You've been married for nine years and have known each other for about … twelve. I was your maid of honor at the wedding. My hair was longer then—I had gorgeous waves. And I wore a stunning red dress …" *Was I there too? Did I have a dress of some sort? Elly, Elly, Elly …*

My parents soon showed up, and we hugged and exchanged greetings.

"Eric is on his way," said Dad. "He had to find parking." We all chatted for a bit, and then Eric tapped on the door and peeked inside.

"Come on in," Mom said.

"Hi, sweetie," said Eric.

"Hi." I replied. *Eric is a handsome piece of something.* Tall, charismatic, intelligent—he was the whole package. *Ahh, the package …*

"We should all get going," said Dad. Then my doctor, neurologist actually, asked to speak with everyone outside of the room. The door wasn't fully closed, so I was able to hear bits and pieces. She asked them to be patient with me and let me take my own time to get back into the swing of things. She also said that I'd be meeting with a therapist weekly to help with the memory and recovery process. Amnesia is a rare condition, she explained, I could start to remember some things, or never remember anything, and they needed to be prepared for either outcome. She told them I hadn't lost motor skills or the knowledge of what things are, how they work, etc., just a block of memories from my past. I'd very likely be remembering things from today forward. This was helpful to me because I hadn't had enough time to search the Internet for "amnesia" to figure out what I was supposed to be doing and not doing. So my plan was to say little and observe a lot while I figured out my next move.

Everyone came back into my room, and my neurologist reminded me of my first appointment with the therapist for next week. *That'll be interesting. I'm going to have to prepare for that one.* We all walked toward the hospital elevator, and I whispered to Elly, "You're coming with me, right?"

She replied, "Sure."

The drive home was funny. I sat in the back between Mom and Elly. Eric drove, and Dad rode shotgun. As I gazed out the window, Eric kept looking at me in the rearview mirror; Elly and Mom were doing the side-glances, and Dad just conspicuously turned his entire body around every few minutes. Finally, I said, "What, old man?" And everyone laughed. That broke some of the quiet tension.

It was a *long* twelve-minute drive home. I remained pretty quiet, and I figured they were all wondering what I was thinking and if anything looked familiar to me, but they didn't want to say too much just yet. *I was glad they had just been reminded that no one was going to want me to regain my memory more than me, and they should remember that if they got frustrated.*

"We're home," Eric said.

It was a chilly January afternoon, but there was no snow on the ground, and the temperature was bearable. I looked up at our high-rise, which was an ultra-modern condo building, and then I looked across the street. I could feel all of them watching me. Our block was clean, and it remained quiet for the most part during the winter months. There were a lot of retailers and restaurants a couple of blocks away that drew in heavy foot traffic in the summer.

"Ready, sweetie?" asked Eric. I nodded and took his extended hand. As we walked into our building, he handed the car keys to Jack, our doorman, for the valet. I love Jack and was about to greet him by name, but then I remembered *not* to remember him.

"Is he going to drive your car?" I asked Eric.

Surprised by my question, Eric said, "No, he—well, yes. He's just going to park it for us."

"Oh, okay," I said and turned to Jack. "Thank you." Then I gave Jack a hug, which surprised him and everyone else. I saw the reflections of their expressions in the mirrored wall as I entered the elevator. I looked at my watch to keep from laughing.

Once we got upstairs, I walked straight to the sofa and sat down. Everyone else slowly made his or her way into the living room. I assumed they'd been chatting about me in the foyer.

"Are you hungry, honey?" Dad asked.

"No, I'm fine. Thank you. Dad." I could tell that he needed me to call him Dad. He lit up.

"Your brothers and your sisters want to know if they can come by with the kids and see you this evening," Mom asked while looking at her cell phone.

"My—how many?" I asked.

Mom grabbed her mouth and began apologizing. "I'm so sorry. I—"

"It's okay. Really, it's okay. It's fine, really. That's how I'm going to remember, by asking questions. It's okay."

"I forgot that quickly," she said.

"Hey, so did I." Everyone chuckled, and I could see that she felt a little better.

"Well, you have three brothers and two sisters. Stewart is your older brother. Then there's your sister, Lisa and your other sister, Tina. Tina moved to Pennsylvania last year for a job. And Stewart lives in California with his family. You're the baby girl. And then there are your twin younger brothers, Carl and Charles, who visited you in the hospital. You have ten nieces and nephews, but I won't go into all of their names right now. That may be too much."

Too much indeed.

My sister's divorces brought them even closer together, and they eventually started to treat me like the married outsider. I soon stopped coming around, and they didn't seem to mind. And when success came for Eric professionally—and my mother bragged about him daily— the wedge in my relationship with my sisters grew even more. Then Tina moved to Pennsylvania "for a job"—job must be code for "another loser dude." *Tina, Tina, Tina.*

So, when my mother said that my sisters wanted to come by, I wondered where she got that. I also wondered why my Aunt Janet wasn't at my place with everyone.

I was closest to my brothers now. I got *even closer* to them when I had fallouts with my sisters. The younger ones were always in my pocket, though. Chuck would come to "have lunch" with me at work, only to ask me for a loan halfway through the meal for some new endeavor, and then have to leave before the check came. That happened at least four times. *Okay, maybe that's my fault, then.* And Carl was at least more of a gentleman when hitting me up for cash. He'd visit me at home — only after first ensuring that Eric wasn't there — and then he'd cook before asking me for rent, car note, or dine-the-latest-hottie money. I'd given him money for each of those at least a dozen times in the last couple of years. *Probably my fault, too, but if I don't help them, they won't call me either.*

"You know, that may be a bit much for me for today. I already have a room of people staring at me," I said.

"Yeah, you're right. That may be too much," said Mom.

Elly walked in from the kitchen carrying a tray of steaming coffee mugs. She handed one to Eric and then placed the tray on the coffee table where the rest of us each grabbed one.

"Thanks Elly. This is delicious," said Eric.

"You're welcome."

"This *is* good. Thank you Elly," I said.

She raised her glass.

After about an hour of random conversation, Mom said, "Maybe we should get going" to Dad.

"We should?" Dad asked, and Mom pointed subtly toward Eric. Then Dad reluctantly said, "Yes, of course." I then walked my parents to the door. Elly and Eric followed suit. We said our good-byes, then I closed the door behind them and walked into the kitchen. I looked in the cabinets and then in the refrigerator, and they were all full of my favorite healthy things like blueberry yogurt, edamame ... caramel ice cream, and chips with salsa. *There are vegetables in the salsa.* Shopping had definitely been done in the last twenty-four hours. I sat at the dining room table. It was weird. I felt as if I'd been gone a long time and, at the same time, as if I'd been gone only a day.

Eric walked back into the apartment. The dining room wasn't immediately visible from the foyer or entrance. I heard him walking toward the bedroom and then back toward the kitchen. He walked through the kitchen and saw me at the table.

"Hi," I said.

"Hi." He sat in the chair next to me, took my hand, and just looked at me. *I really love this man, flaws and all.* He caressed my hand, and then he started to cry. No sound, just tears. Many tears.

"I thought I was going to lose you," he said and then put his face in my lap. *I guess he loves me too.*

THE NEXT DAY

I woke up and felt anxious. Then I remembered that this wasn't my old life, and I didn't have to jump out of bed to get a million things done. I hadn't been in the hospital that long, well conscious anyway, but I got used to being there and had actually begun to feel comfortable there.

Eric wasn't in the bed, but he had been. Then I heard footsteps, and Eric came in, *bearing fruit.*

"Good morning, sweetie," he said, placing a plate of fruit and toast with a cup of tea on my nightstand. It was a sweet gesture, but all I could think about was having the place to myself and hoping he was going to work soon.

"Aw, thank you, Eric."

"You're welcome." He sat on the edge of the bed. "I'm about to head to work, but your cell phone is right here with a speed-dial list of the phone numbers you usually call. Call me if you need anything at all. I'll pop in at about one o'clock. But it'll likely be six or seven before I get home for the day. I really wish I didn't have to leave, but I'm working on a big project."

"Yeah? What do you do?"

Eric went on to tell me that he was a scientist, in R&D mainly, currently working on a groundbreaking asthma drug. As much as he loved to boast, he was being unusually modest today. He was brilliant, though, when it came to advancements in human health and research. He consulted for large pharmaceutical companies and owned over fifty patents. Every major pharma company had offered him a job, but he preferred to remain a consultant. He was easily bored and preferred projects that he could throw himself into and then move on to something completely new and different.

We went from talking about work to his telling me how we met, got married, and bought this condo. Thirty minutes later, he realized he was late.

"Yikes," he said. "I better get going. I so wish I didn't have to leave you here today."

"It's okay. I'll be fine. I'm going to spend the day going through those photo albums in the living room."

"Sounds like a good idea. Make sure you take it easy, though." I leaned in to give him a kiss, which caught him off guard. *I understood.* I guessed, technically, I was just getting to know him again. We looked at each other, which just made things even more awkward. He gave me a peck on the forehead then said, "Bye, Bails — Bailey." I just waved.

When Eric left for work, I took a long hot shower then sat in my favorite space in the apartment — my walk-in closet. *Whoever created the walk-in closet was brilliant.* If it was a man, he must've been under some woman's spell, because no man in his right mind would create such a large space exclusively for retail purchases — *just because.* When I was a kid, I had a standard two-by-four foot closet, which had to be considered abuse. After spending all those weeks in the hospital, I had dropped a few pounds, so today I was able to pick an outfit from the far left of my closet, an area I hadn't been able to pull from in a while. The last time that I did, I was surely testing the seams, but today it fit. I was not one of those people who thought that *small* was the new *large* or *hungry* was the new *sexy*, but I was glad to have gotten rid of my stomach pouch at least. I was healing pretty well; in fact, the only sign that I'd even been in an accident was a small bruise on my head, which my untrimmed bangs partially covered. Speaking of untrimmed, I needed to get my hair and nails done badly. I'd take a walk through the neighborhood later and make some appointments.

I went into the living room and grabbed a couple of photo albums. If asked, at least I could say what I looked at and could make up some real questions. I'd always been a huge picture taker and, once it got even easier with camera phones, my picture taking had reached an all-time ridiculous high. I was getting photos printed for *every* and *no* occasion. Needless to say, there were about ten photo albums from this past year alone on the shelf, and that wasn't even half of them. Looking through the older albums brought back some fun childhood memories.

I was tempted to check my work email to see what had been happening there in my absence. Although I tried to make my job sound more important and harder than it actually was to my family, who thought Eric was saving lives — well, technically he *kinda* did, but that was beside the point — I was pretty much a process manager, so my days were routine. I wasn't in any hurry to get back to work at knirD woN, which was "drink now" spelled backward — the founders were real *nerds* then. I couldn't wait to talk to Christina, my colleague and BFW (best friend at work). We'd started there as interns almost ten years before and were now both managers. Well, she was now a senior manager on track to be a director. I would be as well if I hadn't switched to the *pretty* track back in the day. My inbox had four hundred and nineteen new email messages. *Yeah ... No, we're not doing this today.* I put my laptop back on the coffee table.

I should email Christina.

At least a quarter of all of my flowers in the hospital were from her and my friend Bryce. Most of the other flowers were from work people. As much as I didn't *love* my job, it defined me. Well, I let it define me. The perks and respect that came with it got me out of bed in the morning and helped fill my wine glass in the evening.

It's crazy, but I need to get back there ... eventually.

If I emailed Christina, would I freak her out? I wasn't sure if she knew about the "amnesia." Maybe I could just thank her for the flowers. No, I'd wait. I needed to call her or see her in person.

I put on a little makeup and then put a larger bandage on my head, larger than was actually needed to remind anyone I knew and came in contact with. Then I grabbed my coat, sunglasses, and handbag and headed out the door.

AW, YOU SHOULDN'T HAVE

There weren't many people out and about, since it was the middle of the afternoon on a weekday. I walked across the street to my favorite boutique, Alexis, *one of my favorites anyway.*

I'd spent many, many hours and many card swipes there since they moved into the neighborhood a few years earlier. They knew me all too well.

"Hello," I said as I walked in and moved my sunglasses to the top of my head.

Gasp! "Oh my goodness, you're back," said Angela, the boutique's co-owner. "Ally!" she called out to her sister and co-owner. "You've got to see who just came in."

I stood next to Angela while she inspected me. Angela loved fashion and picked the most gorgeous items for the store, but never wore anything they sold. She was an attractive, tall, plus-size woman who wore a black shirt and slacks every day.

Ally came out and placed her hand over her mouth.

"Right!" said Angela.

"How are you? Oh my goodness, I can't believe you're here. Is it true that you were in a coma—and have *amnesia?*" asked Ally.

"Ally!" Angela said and hit Ally's arm.

"It's okay," I said. "Yes, they say I have amnesia. I'm just out for some fresh air and saw a few nice items in your window."

"Do you remember this place?" Angela asked.

"How's she going to remember it, if she has amnesia?" Ally said.

Angela shrugged.

"No, I don't remember much. But your dresses are gorgeous," I replied.

"You have done some *damage* in this place," Ally said.

"Yes, you definitely have. In a good way," Angela chimed in. I guess my facial expression gave her the impression that I didn't understand her. I was actually looking past her at a delicious red dress on the rack.

"I can see why. I'd love to try on that dress over there," I pointed to the red dress.

"That is so your style. Come on, I'll get it for you," said Angela, and we walked to the rack. "What size are you again?" I raised my shoulders to indicate that I didn't know.

"Let me check our books," said Ally. "I think she's a six, but you look thinner now. Give her a six and a four, but I don't think the six is going to fit." Ally was a spitfire. Unlike her sister, she wore everything in the store. She loved to talk and only allowed you to get half of your sentence out before she responded. She had a slight British accent from spending *a summer* in London. It was comical and inconsistent. After

Paris, New York is known for fashion, so she'd do much better from a business perspective sounding like a New Yorker—as she did *last spring.*

Angela grabbed the two sizes and walked me to the dressing room where she hung them both inside.

"Thank you, Angela." *Oops! Oh good, she's wearing a name tag. I need to be more careful, though. Faking amnesia isn't easy. I* tried on the size four, and it fit like a glove. *I am so buying this.* Then there was a knock on my dressing room door—and Ally handed me another blue dress.

"You're going to love this one too. We ordered them both with you in mind," she said as she hung it in the dressing room.

"Thank you!" I tried it on and loved that one as well. I left the dressing room and handed Angela both dresses.

"So what did you think? Did you love them?" Ally asked.

"You must know me well. I love them both. I'll take 'em."

"I thought so!" said Ally.

I handed her my Amex. "What's the total?"

"Three hundred eighty-four dollars even."

"For both?" *I thought the price tags totaled more than that.*

Angela handed me my card and receipt. I reviewed the receipt and saw that the red dress said, "Comp" next to it, and the four hundred and fifty-five dollar amount had "$0 Due" next to it. I looked up at Angela, then she winked and said, "Welcome back." *Wow, I must've spent more money in here than I thought.*

"Oh my goodness. Thank you so much! That was so sweet. Thank you."

"You're welcome," she said and rubbed my arm as if I were a child. I didn't like that. Ally looked over Angela's shoulder at the screen and looked puzzled. She whispered something in Angela's ear. Angela shook her head. Then they both turned around, and I heard her whisper, "Don't worry, her husband will pay for it."

Was she talking about me? No, they must've been talking about something else. Right? I buy my own clothes.

I took the garment bags, and Ally said, "I'm sure you'll be back in here shopping again in no time." *She was so right.* I frequented that place more than I did the supermarket. I wish I'd been exaggerating. I was a horrible wife when it came to grocery shopping—a stylish, horrible wife.

Then Ally asked, "How's that friend of yours, *Elly*?"

Sidebar. Ally was the ex-wife of Elly's current husband. She *hated* Elly. If the husband had a system, his next spouse would be Illy, then Olly and then Ully—which would be salacious since "Olly" was a man's name. *I digress …*

"Um, okay I guess," I said. "She visited me in the hospital."

"Right," Ally replied. *Awkward.* "That Elly … is a real piece of work. You'll see."

I believe all bitter ex-wives would say the same.

Not knowing how to respond, I just raised my brows and then Ally headed to the back.

As I started to head out, Ally's daughter, Tulip (*I know, right*), walked into the store. Ally's daughter was … a horrible human being. She was rude, dishonest, and ridiculously spoiled. I never knew how her mother allowed it. *I think she overcompensated for being the only parent in the house.* Anyway, as soon as I reached for my sunglasses, Tulip was right at the register with a miserable expression on her face, after dumping her book bag at the entrance.

"Hi, sweetie. How was school?" Angela asked.

"I'm hungry; is my mom here?" Tulip replied. *Isn't she just precious?*

"She's in the back. Say hello to Ms. Bryant." Tulip looked me up and down. "She just got out of the hospital after an accident." Then she whispered loudly, "And she has amnesia."

Tulip's face suddenly brightened up. "Oh, Ms. Bryant. Yes, you were in here last month, and you ordered twenty boxes of cookies from me. I've been holding onto them for you," Tulip said with a mischievous grin. *This lying little snot-ass! I ordered zero boxes of cookies.*

"Are you sure it was me?" I asked. She caught me off guard with this, and I didn't know how to respond.

"It was definitely you, but *you wouldn't remember*," she replied with her "ha ha!" face. Then her mom came out from the back and greeted Tulip. This was my chance to bail.

"Thanks again, ladies," I said and began my departure.

"What about the cookies?" Tulip asked.

"What cookies?" Ally chimed in.

"She ordered twenty boxes of cookies from me last month—for her office or something. I was just wondering when she was going to pay for them. The cookies are in, and you can pick them up here tomorrow."

This little lying heifer! I gotta hand it to her, though, she's good. I looked at Ally and then at Angela who didn't say anything, but were both likely thinking about the *complimentary* designer dress they just gave me.

"Of course. And what's your name, sweetie?" I asked.

"It's Tulip." She said it as if she really wanted to say, "It's Tulip, bitch."

"And how much will the twenty boxes of cookies be?"

"One hundred ten dollars. Five dollars a box and then ten dollars for processing."

I've got her processing. I'm sure that's an "LOL fee" going straight into her pocket. "Well, I'll be sure to stop by tomorrow to pick up the cookies, and I'll have a check for you too. Tulip." *Okay, I'll stop saying her name.*

"Good. Mom, I'm hungry." And just like that, she dismissed me and went on to harass the next adult in line.

I left the store before I ended up having to contribute toward the little crook's prison-prevention trust.

After being hoodwinked, I decided to forgo stopping by the hair salon. When I got back home, I sat in the kitchen where I'd left my cell phone, which desperately needed to be charged. I had text messages from everyone under the sun: Eric, my parents, Elly, my friend Bryce, and a reminder about my therapy appointment. Eric had called and texted me several times, so I called him back but got his voice mail. I guess he worried after not hearing back from his "wife with amnesia" who was back at home for the first day, alone, and not answering her phone. *Oops.*

"Hi, Eric. Sorry, I forgot my cell phone at home when I went for a walk around the neighborhood. I'm just seeing your missed calls and text messages. Anyway, I'm fine, but my phone is about to die. Talk to you later."

I looked at my dresses and was pleased until I remembered that a middle school kid had just bamboozled me. *Ugh.*

Elly's text said that she'd wanted to have lunch with me. *Man, I wish I didn't miss that.* So I gave her a call, and she was actually working from home, so I asked for her address to pay her a visit. Though she lived only ten minutes away, she was nervous about me traveling to her place by myself, but I assured her that I'd be fine. She reluctantly agreed, and then I was on my way.

When I got to her building, there was no one manning the door, so I walked right in and entered the elevator. I knocked on her door and heard her running toward it.

"Hi!"

"Hi! See, I made it okay."

"You did, you did. Come on in." I walked into her apartment, and it smelled like dessert.

"Your place is so nice." *It was gorgeous.*

"Oh, thanks."

"Are you baking something?"

"No, those are candles. Doesn't it smell like the real thing?"

"Yes, but now I want some apple pie."

"I'm sorry. Let me see what I have in the kitchen."

"No, no. I'm kidding. Sit, it's okay. How are you?"

She sat back down. "Me, who cares? I'm fine. How are you? Already out and about—you are something else."

"I couldn't just sit at home. I did spend a couple of hours going through photo albums, though. It was nice. Then I walked the neighborhood and — oh, I think a little girl conned me."

"What little girl?"

"There's a boutique up the street from me —"

"Alexis. Yeah."

"Yeah, well the owner's daughter, I think —"

"Orchid? Lily — no wait … it's something stupid. She is evil. What did she do?"

"She said that I ordered twenty boxes of cookies from her some weeks ago and that I owe her over a hundred bucks for them. This was immediately after her aunt told her that I had amnesia. Would I have ordered twenty boxes of cookies?"

"Hell, no! You don't even like her. Plus, you're always buying candy, plants, books, and junk from your own nieces and nephews. I don't know how you manage to finance your shoe addiction. Don't you pay that little crook a dime." We talked for a while and then she brought out a couple of photo albums.

"Oh, is this your husband?" It was a photo of her and Robert on vacation.

"Yeah, that's my Robby. I've been spending his money on handbags *all* morning online instead of working." She turned the page and didn't say anything more about him. They'd been having a tough time for the last few months. He was never even around anymore. I felt bad for her. But she seemed unmoved by it all. *I don't know.* When they first got married, he wanted to have kids; she wanted to wait and then, when they tried to conceive last year, she couldn't. That may have caused him to resent her.

What sucks was that she put off kids for her accounting career, which ended up taking off and then plummeting. I heard that she helped wealthy people find ... *dishonest* ways to avoid paying taxes. After getting tons of referrals from the rich friends of her clients, she opened her own firm. Then the IRS busted one client of hers after another, and she was done. Her reputation was tarnished—again, I'd heard. She never told me any of this, and I didn't want to believe this about my best friend. She was unemployed for a while—she called it "taking a break"—before accepting a job making a lot less money just to "have something to do outside of the house." Luckily her husband—two decades her senior—was a wealthy businessman. *Of course, that's why she married him.* Right before my accident, she hadn't been talking much about Robert, work, or wanting to have kids anymore. She shopped a lot, though. *That's one of our common denominators.*

"How are you two doing?" I had to see what she was going to say.

"Oh, we're fantastic. He's traveling for business right now. Oh, I want to show you something." *Umm hmm, anything to change the subject. He seemed to always be "away for business" lately.* I followed her to the den then to some art on the wall. I tried not to alter my expression. I'd bought this painting for her when we took a trip to Paris together after college. The whole room was Paris-inspired. The pillows on the chairs, the accessories on the desk, the vase—we shopped for all of it while in Paris.

"This is beautiful."

"You bought it for me."

"I did?" Life was so much simpler back then. We had just graduated from college, had great jobs lined up, had great boyfriends, and had gone to Paris. It was a simpler time — before the absentee husbands, hateful sisters, and job *situations*.

"Yeah, we took a trip to Paris together after college. We also bought this there and …" She showed me everything in the room that we'd bought there and told me the stories and adventures behind each piece.

"Wow, Elly. Do you have photos from our Paris trip?"

"Absolutely." She took me back into the living room. We went through those photo albums and then college photo albums. I thought of correcting her twice during her storytelling because her versions weren't, well, how they really happened. But I had to let it go, even though she was the *best* and *everything good* in *every* story. *I couldn't blow my cover.* One particular story was of a guy I dated my sophomore year that she just referred to as "Ugly Justin" and said, "I can't believe you dated him." Now, after I dated Justin for a year — and dumped him — I learned from a mutual friend that Elly was infatuated with him the summer prior, but he turned her down. He asked me out the following semester. She didn't know that I knew this, though.

We heard a beep, and Elly grabbed her phone. "I have to take this. Excuse me," she said and headed quickly to her kitchen. I heard whispers, giggles, and then more whispers. I continued to look through the albums while she was away — for eight full minutes. *She is working from home — maybe it's work related.*

After all the fun, photos, and reminiscing today, I wanted to tell Elly that I didn't actually have amnesia. I felt bad keeping my best friend in the dark. She of all people would understand why I lied, and I trusted her. *Maybe I'll tell her today.*

"Sorry about that," Elly said, as she came back into the living room with snacks.

"No worries. I know you're working from home. Work comes first," I said. "I'm thinking about possibly going back to work in a couple of weeks myself."

"Listen to me," she said. "You should take your time going back to work. What's the rush? It's like the reset button of your life has been pushed. Appreciate it."

I just nodded. *I should tell her the truth.* "Elly —"

"Wait … I forgot to stop the microwave!" She ran into the kitchen.

"Is everything okay?" I yelled.

"Yeah. The desserts are ruined, though."

"That's all right." As I sat there, I wondered how she was going to react when I told her the truth. *What if she gets mad at me?*

Elly walked back into the living room and plopped herself on the sofa. "I'm sorry. I know you have a sweet tooth."

"Oh, that's okay."

"What were you going to say?"

"Hmm?"

"Before I went into the kitchen you were going to say something."

"Oh, um. I don't remember." I couldn't do it. I don't know why, but it didn't feel like now was the right time. *I'll know when the time is right.*

THERA-PISSED

Today I had my therapy session, and I was nervous. I was afraid I'd say the wrong thing and he'd see right through me. I wish I didn't have to go, but my neurologist recommended it, and my family really wanted me to do it to help with my memory. It was also required before she'd give me clearance to return to work, but ... *I don't want to go back to work just yet. Hmm ...*

While Eric lay in bed next to me, I rubbed his arm and moved closer to him. He turned to face me then he kissed me on my forehead before he hopped out of bed. It's been a week since I returned home, and he hasn't touched me or looked at me in that way. The first night or two I understood and didn't expect it really. I was still a bit sore and getting re-acclimated to being home, he must've thought anyway. Up until a few months ago, we were having adult fun almost every night, but then it slowed down when a project of his got demanding, and he was getting home later.

"Can't you spend a few more minutes with me in bed?" I asked him as he stood in front of his dresser.

"I, um, have a few things to do before we head out," he said then left the room before giving me an awkward grin.

"Okay."

I'd never had to ask him to join me in bed in the past. We'd always had a decent relationship but, given my "condition," I guessed it was taking time to get that piece of it back to normal for some reason.

Maybe I'll make a move tonight instead of waiting for him.

He was taking me to my therapy session, and I definitely didn't want him to sit in on it with me. I needed him to see me as the *pre-accident*, normal me. Plus, I'd mess up what I said for sure if he was in the room. *Maybe I should just take a taxi there by myself. Damn, I'm already sweating.*

"Bailey, do you mind if we leave for your therapy session a little early? I have to meet my brother at one o'clock," Eric asked as he peeked into the bedroom. Eric and his brother, Scott, were very close. Scott was younger and they resembled each other but, between the two, Eric definitely looked like the *after photo* of Scott, if you know what I mean. Scott had let himself go.

"I can just take a taxi. You don't need to take me."

"Are you sure? I don't mind."

"I know. It's okay, though. I've been getting around okay."

"Okay, if you're sure."

"I'm sure."

"Thanks, Bails." Then he pecked me on my forehead and left. *Forehead again? This has got to change.*

I searched the bottom of the closet for wedges and I came across a small Neiman Marcus shopping bag.

What is this?

I reached into the bag and pulled out a box that had a Post-it note on it: "For Elly's b-day." *Oh, yeah.* I'd bought this jewelry box for her months ago. I remember she mentioned that she loved it when we were last at Neiman's. *Wait, today is the fifth — today is Elly's birthday!* I'd spoken to her nearly every day, and she didn't even mention it, or birthday plans, or anything. And she was big on birthdays — especially hers. *Why hadn't she said anything?* She was supposed to be helping me remember things, so this would be the perfect thing for us to do together again. *Hmm … This is weird.* It must have been because of the amnesia. She didn't want to bring it up because of that, but it didn't make sense. *Man, I should've told her the truth. I should call her. No, I'll take the gift to her after my appointment.* She wouldn't be home, so it would be a nice surprise at her door when she got home from work. *I can say that I saw in my datebook that today was her birthday.* Then we could chat about it and maybe even still grab dinner. I should pick up a card too. *I better get going.*

The waiting area of the therapist's office was very modern. It didn't look like troubled souls were spilling their guts on the other side of the wall. I felt so uncomfortable because I didn't know what to expect. I'd never been to a therapist before — *who wanted to be vulnerable with a stranger?* Now I had to go to one and act the whole time. "Acting" sounded better than "lying" … *I know that I'm in denial. Ugh, I can't wait for this to be over. I hope he doesn't think this gift is for him.*

"Mrs. Bryant?"

"Yes. Hi."

"Hi, I'm Dr. Reddy." He gently shook my hand.

"Hi, nice to meet you." *Gulp. Okay, here we go.*

"Pleasure. This way please." *It's show time.* I followed him through the super-modern door, down the ultra-posh hallway and into an incredibly serene room where everything was white, mint green, and silver. *This is how they get the spillage of the beans. You slip into spa-mode, and then you're mentally butt naked on the couch without a single secret to call your own anymore – except for PINs and passwords.*

"Don't you think so, Mrs. Bryant?"

"I'm sorry, what was that?" *I need to pay attention.*

"It's pretty warm for this time of year?"

"Yeah, it is." *No, it isn't. Why does everyone start conversations with the weather? Who cares? It's warm, it's hot, it's raining, it's chilly. What's conversation-worthy about the weather? I never understood that. Just ask me what you're going to ask me. Okay, I'm nervous.*

"But then again that depends on who's impacted, right?" he asked.

Damn. I really need to pay attention. I just nodded and sat in the most comfy chair in the room, assuming that was where I was supposed to be sitting.

"Is it okay, if I sit here?" I was already sitting, looking out the window with one shoe half-dangling off my foot, so any answer other than yes would be wrong. *Oh, I'm supposed to be paying attention.*

"That's fine. Are you nervous about today?"

"A little. I don't really know what to talk about."

"We can talk about whatever you'd like to talk about." *The reverse psychology. I'm onto you, Dr. Reddy.* I was so sure he had a list of at least thirteen and a half things that must be discussed today. The first page of his notepad was blank, but I was sure the pages underneath were filled with all types of scribblings.

"Do you work with amnesia patients often?"

"I try not to label clients in ways that may hold them back."

Ooo-kay. "So, my having amnesia isn't relevant?"

"No, I'm not saying that. I just think we should … talk. Amnesia aside."

My appointment started at 2:00, and I feel like it's 2:50, but the clock says that it's only 2:00:53. Damn. "Okay," I replied. And then we just sat there and looked at each other. Then I started playing with my watch. *I should get a new watch. I've worn this one with everything for the past two years. There was one at the –*

"So, how was your first week back home from the hospital?"

"You mean, from the hospital where I woke up with *amnesia*?"

"Touché, Mrs. Bryant."

Hee-hee. "It's been fine. I think. I should probably get back to work eventually, though."

"Where do you work?"

Surely that's scribbled on page eight of your notepad. "At knirD woN."

"I see. What are your thoughts about work and what you'll be walking back into?"

"It'll be good to get back at some point and ... um ... work. See my colleagues and do ... my job."

I must've sounded like an idiot. I was trying not to say names or discuss what I did in detail. He asked me several more work-related questions, and I answered them as unassumingly as I possibly could. Then I asked him a real-life question to change the subject.

"Dr. Reddy, today is my friend Elly's birthday. She's my best friend—according to her, my family, photos, *et cetera*. And today I learned that it's her birthday after coming across a note on a gift I bought for her that was in my closet. She and I have spoken almost every day, and she hasn't mentioned it. Why do you think that is?"

"That's interesting. Why do you think she hasn't mentioned it?"

Seriously dude—this is the one question that I actually wanted an answer to. "I have no idea."

"What I mean is, how do you think she should have handled it given the situation?"

"By situation, you mean my amnesia?" I asked and smirked.

"Mrs. Bryant."

I guess he's all out of touchés. "Given the amount of times she and I have spoken and have seen each other leading up to today and with her helping me to remember other things, not mentioning her birthday sounds like the opposite of what she should do."

"So your expectations weren't met?"

"Never mind."

"Are you getting frustrated?"

"Nope." I remained quiet. He didn't like that.

"The reason that I ask about your expectations is because it's going to be an integral ..."

He continued, but I'd officially tuned him out. Everything was going according to plan. *I really like this nail color. I should've written the name of it down. Especially since I may need to find a new nail salon where rumors of me being nuts aren't circulating. You can see the Statue of Liberty from here. This view rocks!*

"Mrs. Bryant!"

"Yes?" *Ding. The clock sounds. And that's our time.* "Thank you for your time, Dr. Reddy." *I'm sure he won't be recommending that I return to work just yet.*

Outside there were people moving, horns honking, and yellow snow on the curb. *This is where I belong.* I hailed a cab and headed to Elly's place. I wasn't sure what Dr. Reddy would communicate to my neurologist about this session, but I managed to avoid any questions from him about my family that could've tripped me up and, hopefully, I'd get another chance to convince him that I wasn't actually crazy, when I was ready to go back to work, that is.

When I reached Elly's building, I saw the doorman at his post looking straight ahead, and I just walked past him to the elevator as I'd done a million times before. I used to wonder why he was even there until I saw him throw a man out last year who tried to slip by him. The doorman wasn't totally useless after all.

I knew that Elly would love this gift. I wished I could have been there when she opened it, but I knew she'd be pleasantly surprised, given my *touché* and all.

When I turned the corner on Elly's floor, I froze—suddenly I felt as though things were moving in slow motion. I was having an out-of-body experience.

Elly was leaning against her door, and Eric was leaning on her, kissing her.

I couldn't move. I couldn't breathe.

Then I was back at the elevator frantically pushing the down button. *What was happening? What the hell was happening?* I got into the elevator, took off my jacket, and tried to breathe. It was taking forever to get to the ground floor. *What did I just see? Did I really just see that?*

When I got out of the elevator, the crisp lobby air hit me in the face. I didn't blink or move. This *did* just really happen. Then I was in front of the building anxiously waving for a taxi.

"Where to?" the driver asked as I entered the cab. I didn't know where to go. I looked back at the building, still hoping that that hadn't just really happened.

"Please take me to Ninth Street," I said, "In Park Slope." I couldn't go home. I needed to get to my parent's house.

I called my parents while en route so as to not freak them out once I got there.

"Hi, Dad."

"Hi, honey. How are you?"

"I'm fine. I just got in a taxi and am coming over."

"Over here?"

"Yes."

"Where are you now?"

"I'm still in the city."

"Do you—Okay. Um, let me give you the address. Tell the cab driver it's 801 Ninth Street."

I repeated, "801 Ninth Street" to appease Dad, and the cab driver just looked at me in the rearview mirror.

"Are you okay?"

"I'm okay. See you soon." I hung up before my voice got shaky.

The cab driver got me to my parents, and I walked up to their front door but couldn't ring the doorbell. So I sat on the front steps and tried to collect my thoughts. I kept replaying what happened, seeing Eric and Elly together in my head. *Kissing. Smiling.* They were dressed up, so *he* must've been her birthday plans. *How long has this been going on? Was she the reason he started coming home late from work months ago?* No wonder she'd become so indifferent about her issues with her own husband—she was busy cavorting with mine.

I couldn't believe I had to deal with all of this right now— how could they? My best friend … I couldn't stop the tears from falling. I was getting anxious, but I couldn't let my parents see me like this. I thought my husband loved me, especially after the accident. He seemed so happy that I'd made it through, so attentive and … *So … not having sex with me.*

Wow! That's why he wasn't having sex with me.

Okay, what's my plan? What is the plan? I don't have a plan …

I couldn't tell my parents. Not right now—not as much as my mother loved Eric. Things were so much better now between her and me. *What if she blamed me for his infidelity?* I needed to figure out what to do first. And to think I was considering telling Elly that I didn't really have amnesia. She'd been like a sister to me. Now I felt as though I did have amnesia. Nothing was as I thought it was. I always thought that if something of this magnitude would ever happen to me, I'd be at Elly's, crying on her shoulder.

I was getting cold and needed to go inside before one of my parents saw me and came outside. I stood up, got myself together, and hoped there weren't any guests over.

Dad opened the door. He must've seen me through the window. "Bailey — come in, come in," he said as he pulled me into an embrace.

"Hi Dad." I hugged him tight. *Just what I needed.*

We sat on the sofa. No guests were there — *thank goodness.*

"Are you okay?"

"I'm okay." I was about to cry, so I put my head on his shoulder. He put his arm around me, and we just sat there. He rubbed my arm and could sense that that was exactly what I needed. I heard voices in the kitchen and asked, "Are Mom and Aunt Janet in there?"

"Your mom is in there."

"Oh, okay." I assumed she was in there with my Aunt Janet, who was my mom's fashionable older sister. She had moved in with my parents a few years ago when her husband died. *She's awesome.* We were really close, but I hadn't seen her much since I'd been back.

He paused before saying, "She's with your sister, Lisa."

Oh great. The last thing I need right now is for my sister to tell me how much she hates my guts. Maybe I shouldn't have come here. I wanted to cry again.

Lisa was sitting at the table, and Mom was leaning against the kitchen island sipping a cup of tea. When Mom saw me in the doorway, her face lit up. Lisa looked up from her magazine, gave me a *smrown* (smile-frown) and then looked back down before I could even return the half-assed gesture. Mind you, this was the first time she'd seen me since I'd been out of the hospital—assuming that she visited me there. *So much for hoping she'd want to bury the hatchet.*

"Bailey!" Mom screamed when she saw me. She put down her tea, and then I walked right into a warm, tight embrace. *I didn't want to let go. She hadn't reacted to me like that in years.* Then she said, "We would've come and gotten you."

"It's okay. I was out and about and just decided to come and see you two."

She walked me over to Lisa and said, "This is your sister, Lisa."

I leaned in toward Lisa but stopped when she didn't even look up at me. Dad was standing in the kitchen doorway, when Mom said to Lisa, "Do you see your sister? Your sister who almost died!"

"Almost died? She didn't almost anything. She's fine," she said and kept her head down. *Either she's really fascinated by what she's reading, or she's deliberately disregarding me. It's a fashion magazine, and she's wearing a pair of Puma's with brown slacks. You be the judge.*

Mom was about to yell something, but I held her arm and said, "It's okay, Mom." *The issues my sister had with me were not going to be resolved today. And I didn't have the energy for them at all.*

"It's not okay!" Mom said in frustration.

I held her arms again and said, "I'm tired. Can I lie down somewhere?"

Mom redirected her attention to me and said, "Of course, honey. Sure." She held my face to inspect me. I wanted to cry again, so I had to get out of there.

"Show me where to lie down please, Dad." Dad looked sad all of a sudden. He definitely wasn't happy about the state of the relationship between my sister and me. But he couldn't have been sadder about it than I was—especially today. I could have so used the comfort of a sister.

When I was in fourth grade at a new school, and my sisters were in middle school, a couple of older girls were picking on me. I was in my bedroom crying about it one day after school, and my sisters consoled me, which made me feel so much better. They also beat the hell out of the two girls the next day. Those girls never bothered me again. More importantly, my sisters had my back. I would do anything to have that now.

Dad walked me upstairs to the guest bedroom. We passed by the family room, and my favorite niece Olivia was in there asleep. She was the sweetest, smartest little girl any aunt could ask for. It amazed me that she'd spent time in Lisa's womb. Since Olivia got a cell phone, we'd been able to chat at least once a week. Before then, her mother kept us away from each other. *She's jealous that we're so close.*

"Here you go, Bailey," Dad said, as he fluffed the pillows and pulled back the covers on the bed for me.

"Thanks, Dad." I got under the covers. The bed was so soft and smelled like fabric softener. This was perfect.

He pulled the covers over me and said, "Let me know if you need anything." Then he left.

I stared out of the window, as I just lay there trying to make sense of a day that didn't make sense. I heard footsteps in the hall, and Mom entered the room. She placed a plate of crackers and cheese and a cup of tea on the nightstand.

"I thought you might want a little snack," she said as she sat on the bed.

"Thanks, Mom." I put my head in her lap, and she caressed my face. Then I began to cry. I couldn't hold it back anymore. I cried and cried some more while Mom held me, rocked me and consoled me.

"Bailey what is it? What's wrong?" I heard the worry in her voice—then I saw Lisa in the doorway. She looked over at me before walking away.

It was dark now, and the street lights were on, so several hours must have passed. *I actually got some sleep.* I looked around and saw I was in my parent's house, so I knew the day wasn't a dream. I shifted in the bed and noticed someone in the bed with me. *Olivia.* She was lying there, awake and holding my hand.

"Hey there," I said.

"You remember me, Aunt B?"

Oh, yeah. "Yeah, I saw some photos and a family video. You were in them."

Olivia put her head on my shoulder and put her arm across me. "When I woke up, Grandma told me that you were here but you were sleeping, so I asked my mom if I could stay."

What? My sister allowed Olivia to stay behind to see me? There has to me more to that story. But I won't dig any deeper for now. I just said, "I'm glad you're here."

"Me too."

A little later, Olivia and I went downstairs. *Something smelled delicious.* My parents were in the kitchen, and my Aunt Janet was here — *Yay!* When Aunt Janet moved in, she fully renovated my parent's basement and made it her own gorgeous sanctuary. When her husband died, he'd left her quite a bit of money, so she bought herself whatever she wanted whenever she wanted. She was a free spirit who lived by her own rules and had always been the *fun aunt.*

"My girls are up," Dad said.

Olivia headed straight to my aunt who fed her preview bites of whatever she'd been cooking.

"Hi, everybody," I said.

"Bailey B," said Aunt Janet and hugged me tight. *We're quite the hugging family.*

My aunt began to inspect me by holding my face in her hands. I pulled away before she found something to be concerned about. *Too late.*

"You lost weight in the hospital," she said.

"Well, we have the prescription to fix that right here," Dad replied.

"Good because I'm very hungry," I reassured her. *She already thinks that I don't eat enough on purpose.* "What time is it anyway?"

"It's 10:20," said Olivia.

"Wow. I slept a long time."

"You did. You were exhausted—physically and mentally," Mom said, and she looked at me again with concern in her eyes. Dad was looking at me the same way. She must've told him about my little breakdown. *I can't bring them in on what's going on. Not yet. But it's great that my mom is concerned.*

"Well, I'm sure a good meal will fix me," I replied, but they weren't buying it. Their stares were unmoved. "What are you drinking, sweetie?" I asked my niece in an effort to change the subject.

"Iced tea," she replied and handed me her cup. I drank her iced tea, and my parents and aunt got back to preparing the food.

"Come set the table with me?" I said to Olivia.

"No, Aunt B, I'll do it," she replied and tapped my shoulder, as she walked out of the kitchen and into the dining room. *If my other nieces and nephews were half as sweet as she is, the entire northern hemisphere would be a better place.*

As I sat at the kitchen table, my parents kept sneaking peeks at me.

I hope they don't think I'm losing it. "Question," I said. "Why did Lisa respond like that to me earlier?"

"Well …" said Dad.

"Um …" said Mom.

"She doesn't like you," said Aunt Janet.

"Janet!" said Dad.

"It's true," said Aunt Janet. "You all were close, now you're not. Tina doesn't like you, either. They said you used to brag too much and acted better than them. But they were just jealous, if you ask me."

"No one *asked you*. Let's pour this out, okay?" Mom said and dumped Aunt Janet's large goblet of wine in the sink. Aunt Janet shrugged and continued *stirring the pot* ... on the stove. Then it was quiet.

"Where did I leave my cell phone?" I asked in an effort to break the tension.

"In the living room on the sofa," Dad said.

"Thanks." I had a few missed calls, texts, and some new email. My phone was also dying, so I took my charger and headed to the dining room where my niece was setting the table. I found an outlet to charge my phone.

"How many people are eating dinner?" She had set plates for six people.

"Oh," she replied. "Just the five of us." Then took one of the place settings away.

Good. I thought my sister was coming back. "Do we always eat this late?"

"No. I think Grandma started cooking earlier, but you were asleep, so they waited for you to get up."

"Gotcha." I hadn't had dinner at my parents in a while, so I didn't know how late they ate anymore. "So what have you been up to these days?"

"Well, I took my PSATs and am reviewing colleges now, so I'm excited about that."

"Good job! What's your top choice school?"

"Honestly, whichever one gives me the most scholarship money. And is preferably not local. I *really* want to go away."

I'd want to get away from her grumpy mom, too. "Don't worry about cost," I said. "We're going to get you to wherever you want to go. Your grades are good, right?" *They were great.*

She proudly said, "They are, Aunt B. I have a 3.8 grade point average."

"Of course you do." I was so proud. "So cost aside, what's your top choice?"

Olivia grinned but didn't answer.

"Is it my alma mater?"

"It's on the list. It's in the top three."

"Yes!" I replied a bit too loudly. Dad hurried into the dining room, looked at the two of us, and went back to the kitchen. Then Olivia asked, "Wait, Aunt B, you remember where you went to college?"

Fair question. "Yeah, I have alumni mugs, calendars, and pens all over my place. I've been Inspector Gadget all week piecing together many details of my life."

"Inspector who?"

"Never mind." *Generation gaps.*

"Dinner is ready!" Dad sang from the kitchen.

My parents set the food on the dining room table. I went into the kitchen to get a pitcher of iced tea, but my aunt beat me to it. *She was staring at me weirdly.* We all sat down. Dad said the grace, and then we all had a great dining experience. We all talked as if everything were normal again. Maybe it was—here anyway. Then my cell phone vibrated. *A text message from Elly.* My entire mood changed.

"Is that Eric?" Dad asked.

"No, it's not. Do you mind if I stay here tonight? It's late."

"Of course we don't mind. We called Eric when you were sleeping and told him that you were here."

"Thanks."

"Are you okay?" Mom asked. She could tell that I was totally somewhere else.

"I was about to ask the same thing," said Aunt Janet.

"Yeah, I'm fine."

A couple of days had come and gone, and I was still at my parent's house. Now it was Sunday, and I spent most of the day in bed watching television and sleeping. Dad brought me breakfast in bed, and my niece cuddled with me while I slept, and laughed with me while watching a marathon of *Modern Family*. Eric had left me a couple of voice messages. The sound of his voice made me want to throw my phone through the window to Manhattan and strike him right in the center of his throat. *I've progressed from sadness to anger. I believe the next phase is violence, if I remember correctly.*

Mom joined Olivia and me in the bedroom.

"Your Aunt Janet said that you two were going to go out today, and then you changed your mind."

"Yeah, I thought she wanted to go to shopping, and then she started talking about some yarn expo. So I got tired."

"You got tired?" Mom asked and tilted her head.

"Yeah, the thought of a convention center full of yarn instantly made me tired. No department stores? What happened to Aunt Janet?"

"She has new interests, that's all."

"I don't like her new interests. Does this mean that we're all getting knitted items for our birthdays?"

Mom chuckled and said, "I don't know, Bailey."

"She said that they have the expo on Sundays now because of traffic. I told her that they have the expo on Sunday because it's yarn."

Olivia giggled, and Mom shook her head.

"Did I hurt her feelings?" I asked.

Mom just shrugged.

"Was I the *yarn expo type* in the past?"

"Well, no. She just wanted to spend some time with you."

Now I felt bad. *She is my favorite aunt.* "I'll make it up to her. I hardly want to be out at all—yarn was not the magic word to get me to hop out of bed." *Maybe if I do something with her, it will end her staring at me all weird.*

Later that evening, my brother Carl came over, and he and I took a walk around the neighborhood. It was good to see him, get some fresh air, and take my mind off things.

"So, when did you move to Connecticut?" I asked him.

"Right after Christmas," he said and coughed. "I'm just getting over a cold."

"Aw." I tightened the scarf on his neck. "Where did you live before that?"

"Oh, I was a couple miles from here actually. It's so weird … that you don't remember. Sorry—Mom and Dad told us not to bring it up."

Interesting. "That's okay. What moved you out of Brooklyn?"

"I thought it would be cheaper, but it's costing me more money overall."

Here we go. I'm not falling for that one. Dodge. "Mom said that you're dating someone?"

"Yeah, Sarah. She's great, and she's a singer. I gave Mom one of her CDs. You should listen to it. It's so good."

"Wait, is it the CD on the counter with the blue guitar on the cover?"

"Yeah. Have you heard it?"

"Yes, I did. So that's her … She has another job right?"

"No, she's really pursuing the music."

"Interesting. Have Mom and Dad been out to Connecticut to see your place?"

"Yeah, they came out. I felt bad because I didn't have any groceries. I wanted to make them a nice lunch, but they ended up having to take me out to eat."

Dodge number two. "Oh yeah? That's a beautiful park. I walked through it the other day, and there were tons of people walking their dogs, even though it was cold. Have you been there?"

"Yeah. We all used to play there growing up."

"Oh."

"Come on. Let's walk through it for old time's sake."

"Okay." I had hoped that my changing the subject and reminding him that things had changed would be an indicator that it's not always about *Carl*. It was great walking through the park with him, though. We passed by where I had taught him how to ride a bike.

"Hey, you taught me how to ride a bike, and I had my first fall-free ride right here."

I smirked and said, "I can picture that. I saw some photos of you when you were younger. Why did you always have dried snot on your face?"

"Hey, I was a kid," he said and snickered. "Blame the adults and *older siblings* who were around me."

"Umm hmm."

He *sniffled* and I peered into his nostrils. He tried to move me out of the way.

"Keep it in there, snot man. It's shiny. I see it!" I said.

He snorted and then, like clockwork, a big snot bubble exploded out of his nose. Neither of us could contain our laughter. I gave him all of the tissues in my pocket.

"This is all your fault!"

"Just clean your face!"

After he threw the used tissues in the trash, I tried to hold his arm, but he pushed me away because I wouldn't stop laughing.

"Okay, okay," I said.

Then we walked arm in arm while we *both* tried not to laugh. We were a block away from my parents' place when Carl said, "I hate to ask, but I could really use a loan."

Really Carl? Money from your amnesia'ed sister? "Yeah, what for?"

"My expenses are crazy. Rent is cheaper, but now I need a car to get anywhere and—"

"I'm sorry. I can't help you."

"Oh."

"Why didn't you account for the expenses before you moved out there?" *Surely there's an app for that. And you are twenty-nine years old!*

"I did but … I don't know."

"Mom and Dad have tons of room if you need to crash with them while you figure things out."

"I can't move in with them. I'm twenty-nine years old."

"That's a good point." *One that went over his head, unfortunately.*

"So, you can't loan me some funds just until I get an additional job or something?"

Or something meaning ask me for an additional loan in the future. "No, I can't. I have too many uncertainties right now."

"I understand. I'll check back with you in a couple of weeks."

Are you freakin' kidding me? "Actually, you should *not* check back with me in a couple of weeks. I cannot help you, Carl."

He was surprised and stopped in his tracks. *Yeah, this is the new me – get used to it and spread the word!* The last block to my parent's was quiet. He patted my arm at the door and was on his way before I knew it. I watched him walk down the street wondering if he'd delete my number from his phone. That wasn't fun at all. I was more comfortable being a pushover. I was tempted to call his name and just write him a check, but I knew I had to resist if I wanted things to improve. *This must be Lose-Your-Loved-Ones month, and I'm in the lead.*

I leaned against the railing and reminisced about playing on these same streets as a kid with all of my siblings. The neighborhood looked the same. The brownstone-lined street was my safe haven and my parent's warm, food-scented home always welcomed me at the end of each day. My parents had lived there and had been married for forty years … to each other. I finally went back inside and my parents were cooking again. *Too funny.*

I asked my Aunt Janet to ride with me to pick up dessert and then head to my place to get my laptop and some clothes, since Eric was in New Jersey working. She didn't want to drive, which was weird because she loved to drive, and it would've been the most convenient option. In fact, I noticed that I hadn't seen her vintage pink Porsche on the block in a while. I couldn't ask anyone, though, because how would *I* have known that she had one. We ended up taking a taxi and had a great chat. It made me think of how Olivia and I would be when we're older. By the time we got back to Brooklyn, dinner was ready.

DECEPTION

I woke up with head pains that I hadn't experienced since I was in the hospital, so I made an appointment with my neurologist. I didn't want to worry my parents, but they weren't going to let me leave this place alone without telling them where I was going. *I probably shouldn't go alone anyway the way I'm feeling.*

"What's wrong?" Aunt Janet asked when I entered the kitchen. My eyes were bloodshot.

"Just a little headache, that's all."

"Have you taken your prescription today?"

"I'm about to now." I grabbed a bottle of water and downed two pills.

"You should've taken those hours ago. And you should eat something." She went from looking at me weird to avoiding eye contact. *What's up with her?*

"I'll just have some cereal." I prepared a bowl and walked to the living room, as my parents came in from outside giggling like a couple of high school kids.

"Hey," they said in unison.

"Hi. Where are you two coming from?"

"Grocery shopping," said Dad.

"Where are the groceries?" I asked.

"Oh, they have this new delivery service. So they're going to bring them over in the next hour," said Mom.

"Sweet," I said.

"Are you okay?" said Dad.

"Please stop asking me if I'm okay. All of you," I said, then looked at Mom who did it the most. "I just have a little headache. I just took my prescription." *I knew that question was next.*

"Okay," he said.

"Do either of you want to come with me into the city? I'm going to see my neurologist."

"I thought your appointment was at the end of the week," said Mom.

"Yeah ... I just—I called her. I just wanted to pop in and chat with her."

Neither of my parents said anything. *They were onto me.*

"I'll go with you. What time?" asked Mom.

"At 2:30."

"I'll be ready." *I still can't believe my mom is spending time with me. Just like old times; it's been awesome.*

By the time we got to the medical center, I felt better, but I wasn't one hundred percent. The neurologist ran some tests and said that everything looked okay.

"Have you experienced any recent stress?" she asked.

My mother had just gone to the ladies room, so luckily I was able to have an honest conversation without her hearing any of it.

"Yes. I recently learned some disturbing things about someone. It definitely stressed me out."

"Oh, I'm sorry. That was likely what triggered your head pains today then because your scans are clear. But I'm glad that you thought to come in and not ignore it. Tell me, have you been playing over the situation in your head?"

"Constantly."

"Yeah, that's not healthy. Before today, what had you been doing in your spare time?"

"Nothing much actually. Familiarizing myself with people and places. Spending a lot of time with family. My mom set up Skype video calls for me with each of my family members who are out of state."

"That's good, but it'll really help for you to get back to your normal life. I spoke with your therapist last week." *Uh oh.*

"Oh, you did?"

"Yes," she said and looked at me before continuing. "He said the session was interesting, but it would be okay for you to return to work." *What?*

"Oh, okay."

"He said that you appeared nervous and that you weren't forthcoming, but you can return to work, part-time if you prefer."

"Well, that's good then." *Maybe it was what I needed.*

"What are your thoughts about returning to work?"

"Honestly, I was in no hurry, but I think I need the mental stimulation."

"I agree. Maybe start off with three days a week before transitioning to full-time. And I'd like you to continue the therapy sessions too. I've had amnesia patients say that it really helped them with their memory."

"Okay. Could you recommend another therapist, though?" *I'd be embarrassed to return to Dr. Reddy now. I need to turn over a new leaf – a non-crazy leaf.*

"Sure. Did you not like Dr. Reddy?"

"He was okay. I think I'd have a hard time opening up to him, though."

"I see. I think I know just the therapist for you. And she's in mid-town near your job."

"I'll get you her information and set up an appointment for you. Oh, I need you to do something else. You're going to hate this. Get a massage. It'll help with the stress."

"Will do."

A couple of mornings later I lay in bed and attempted to figure out my next steps. I was undecided on when to return to work—oh, and I needed to call Christina. She'd left me a message over the weekend, but I'd been in no condition to speak with anyone. Her family took a few weeks' vacation after Christmas, so she probably just got back in town. And Elly had been calling my cell non-stop and leaving messages. *The bitch wanted to go shopping, see a play, do dinner – do my husband.* I didn't return any of her calls. That was a conversation that I couldn't fake. Then there was Eric. *Ugh.* I didn't know what to do. I didn't want to be the third daughter to get divorced. But I couldn't ignore the fact that he'd been unfaithful. I went from being angry to being scared. I didn't want to be alone and, on a shallower note, I liked the lifestyle that Eric provided. I also didn't like confrontation. I'd never confronted Eric—not when he came home with hungry colleagues without a heads up, bought property in Hoboken *and Canada* without first consulting me, or when he shared details about our marriage with my mother. I'd never said a word.

Like clockwork, my cell phone rang, and it was Eric. I hit the ignore button. He had called me every day, but I'd let it go to voice mail. *There was a knock.*

"Come in."

"What are you up to?" asked Mom.

"Nothing really. Thinking about when I'll return to work."

"When are you thinking?"

"Maybe next week. I'll see."

"As long as you're ready. It's been great having you here though," she said. *Aww, I loved hearing that.* "I don't know how you've been able to stay away from that sweet Eric for so long." *Ugh! She ruined the moment and confirmed that I can't tell her what he did. I'm on my own for this one.*

"I think I'm ready to go back to work." My phone rang again. *Eric.*

"Oh, speak of the devil," Mom said. *So true.* "Look, it's Eric calling." She handed me the phone.

"I can call him back later."

"No, no. I can leave. Go ahead; he's been calling for you." She left and closed the door.

I'm not ready for this. "Hello."

"Bailey? I've been calling you. Are you okay?"

"I'm fine."

"Your parents said that you were sick."

"I'm fine. I was—I'm fine."

"Okay. Why haven't you returned my calls? I've been worried about you."

I started to get upset. *I need to get off the phone.* "I need to go."

"What—what, go where? I'm trying to talk to you. I'm super busy, but I took time to call you—"

"Are you kidding me? What is it, a favor for you to call me?" He had sounded smug, and I lost it.

"That's not what I meant."

"Then what did you mean?"

"What the hell, Bailey? What's gotten into you?"

"What's gotten into me?"

"Yeah."

"Why are you cheating on me? Huh! Tell me that!" *Silence.* "No response?"

"What are you talking about?"

"You know exactly what I'm talking about. I saw it with my own eyes!"

"I don't know what you think you envisioned, Bailey, but maybe you just need to get some rest."

"Are you kidding me? I'm not crazy—I know what I saw!"

"Look," he said in a lower voice. "We can talk about this later. There's been a misunderstanding, obviously. I'll come by later. Just get some rest. Okay?"

"Don't bother!" I hung up and threw the phone on the floor. I heard footsteps, and then Mom peeked in the room.

"Is everything—"

"Not now, Mom." I closed the door and leaned against it before sinking to the floor.

What have I done?

I woke up several hours later with a headache. I sat up in the bed and realized that I'd slept on some chocolate, which was now smudged across my t-shirt. *Great.* My hair was all over the place, so I just gathered it all at the top with a rubber band. I grabbed my prescription and headed downstairs, where I'd heard voices. The conversation stopped when I got about a third of the way down. Eric and my parents were at the bottom looking up at me. I must've been quite a messy sight. I proceeded slowly.

"What's going on?" I asked.

Eric looked down, and then my mother looked at my father.

"How are you feeling?" Dad asked.

"Fine. What's going on?"

Mom cleared her throat and said, "Eric said that you sounded a little confused on the phone earlier."

"Confused?" I asked.

She continued, "We were thinking that maybe it would be a good idea for you to spend a little more time back at the hospital."

"What? I don't need to go back to the hospital. I'm fine," I said. "What the hell did you tell them?"

"Sweetie," Eric said and took my hand.

I pulled away.

"We just want what's best for you," Eric said. We locked eyes.

This bastard wants them to think I've lost it. He's already gotten to them.

Dad touched my shoulder, and said, "Bailey, maybe just for a day. You can get some rest there. That's all." I looked past my parents and saw a small overnight bag by the door.

I can't believe this is happening.

"I don't need to go back. I need my damn husband to tell the truth about what's really going on!" I said. I was beyond furious at this point. I crossed my arms, then put my hands on my hips and crossed my arms again. They were all just staring at me.

"Bailey," my mom said as if I were some stupid confused child. "Truth?"

Eric had already won. My mom especially wouldn't have believed anything negative about him at that moment.

I felt the tears coming, so I went back upstairs. I sat on the bed and stared ahead. *How did I get to this?* Dad tapped on the door.

"Come in."

He sat down next to me and held my hand. "It's okay, honey."

"Dad, I don't know what he told you, but he's lying. I'm okay. He's the one who's dishonest," I said, now crying. "I told him—I told him what I saw. He knows that it's true." I was blubbering and must've sounded crazy for sure. Dad just looked at me, and I saw his eyes well up. *No, Dad!* He held me, and my head fell onto his shoulder.

"Please, let's just go," he said.

The drive back to the hospital was déjà vu. I sat in the backseat with Mom while Eric drove, and Dad was in the passenger seat. I decided not to fight going. I'd already felt defeated and knew I needed to come at this from an angle other than resistance.

When we got there, I was escorted to a nice room after the doctors ran some scans. I sat in a chair, and everyone else stood around while we waited for my neurologist to come. A nurse entered the room.

"Hello. Your regular neurologist, Dr. Harrison, is in surgery, but she'll see you this evening. Feel free to relax and get comfortable until then."

"Okay, thank you," said Mom.

"Let me know if you need anything," said the nurse then left.

The room was quiet and tense.

"You can all go," I said.

"No way. We'll stay with you for a while," said Dad.

"Actually, I do need to leave. I'm so sorry," Eric said, with his faux apologetic expression.

Of course he had to leave. His mission was accomplished.

"Don't be sorry. You've done so much already. Go. We'll stay with her," said Mom. *Done so much already. She's so blinded.*

Eric walked toward me, but my expression stopped him in his tracks.

"I'll come by tomorrow, Bailey," he said, and then he patted Dad's back and walked out with Mom.

Dad sat down next to me. "This is a nice place. Getting away to get some rest isn't so bad."

"It's okay, Dad."

"Want to see what's on TV?"

"Sure."

He flipped through the channels until he came across a Knicks game. "Is this okay?" he asked. He and I had been watching basketball together since I was a little girl.

"Yeah."

The next morning, I was pissed as soon as I realized where I was and why. I dreamt that Elly visited me here and brought black roses. I charged at her, and multiple hospital staff had to hold me down. They ended up sedating me and keeping me for an additional week. *When I woke up, I knew that I had to keep my emotions in check if I wanted to shake the perception that I was losing it.* I called for my nurse.

"Good morning, Bailey. Did you sleep well?"

"Hi. Yes, I did. Will I be seeing Dr. Harrison today?"

She looked at her chart and said, "Yes, she'll be stopping by at eleven o'clock."

"My scans were fine, right?"

"I believe so, but I'll let her discuss that with you."

"Any chance I can meet with her sooner? Her surgery ran over yesterday, so I didn't get to see her."

"I'll go see if she's free now. If not, I'll leave a note in her office."

"Thank you. I appreciate it."

After I freshened up, I noticed my mother's coat in the chair. *Did she stay here overnight? Where is she now?* I peeked into the hall. No one I knew. I got back in bed and skimmed through a magazine. A few minutes later there was a knock at my door.

"Come in."

"Hi, Bailey. How are you feeling?" asked Dr. Harrison.

"I'm fine. Thanks for seeing me early."

"No problem," she said then checked my heart rate and eyes. "So what brought you back in here?"

"My family."

"Yeah, were they worried about something in particular?"

"Is my mother out there?"

"I haven't seen her."

"Can I tell you something in confidence?"

"Of course."

"When I was in here the other day with head pains due to a *stressful situation* —"

"Yeah?"

"I'd just learned that my husband was having an affair. And I saw it for myself, so it wasn't hearsay."

"Oh no, that's awful."

"Well, I confronted him yesterday, and then he got to my parents telling them that I was confused and who knows what else. I wake up from a nap and walk into an intervention, then end up here."

"Oh my God. I'm so sorry. That's just terrible."

"I don't know what they've told you, but I'm not losing it. I'm sure my scans were fine too."

"They were fine. I was going to release you this afternoon anyway. You are, of course, free to go at any time."

"Thank you."

"What are you going to do?"

"I plan to stay with my parents for now and figure it out. I was going to return to work too. Maybe next week."

"That's good. And the therapist will be good for you too. You need an outlet to discuss that … stress. Don't keep it in."

"You're right. Oh, I wanted to ask you. Has my employer been informed about the … um, the amnesia?"

"If you need documentation so that your employer can make workplace accommodations, with the amnesia being treated as a disability, we could provide that for you. Would you need that?" *She was looking at me strangely. Did she know? Could she see right through me?*

"I'd rather not."

"Okay, then." She patted my shoulder and left.

As I gathered my things, Eric walked in.

"Hi," he said and closed the door

"Where's my mother?"

"Look, Bailey," he said and rubbed my arm. "I'm not a perfect man, but I love you. I don't want you to think ill of me."

"It's too late for that, Eric."

"Please, I'll never do anything to hurt you."

"Going forward? Because you've already hurt me."

"I—won't hurt you. I need you. Please sweetie." And then he held me. I didn't immediately pull away; then I remembered that *he* put me back in this place.

I pulled away and said, "What about what you told my parents? You have them thinking I'm crazy when you know—"

"I'd never tell them that you were crazy. I just said that you were probably exhausted. I wanted you to get the care you needed."

"Stop it, Eric. You know that that's not true. This is all because you were unfaithful, and I called you on it. Don't do this." I held my head — *not that that would prevent the pain.*

"I don't want you to get worked up. Come on, let's go home. Everything is going to be fine. It's going to be perfect."

Manipulative bastard. "I'm going back to my parents. I don't—" Mom walked in and smiled when she saw us standing close, assuming that all was well with us.

MY NEW REALITY

I managed to get to the weekend avoiding behaviors and conversations that would have my parents and aunt think I wasn't okay. My mother even made a comment about my seeming better now that I was no longer *exhausted*, so I felt I was in the clear. Eric came by every day, though, which was a challenge. He'd stay for about an hour or two and be charming and nice to my family. I had to act as though I didn't mind his being there, or Mom would wonder what was up with me. What sucked was that when Eric was around, Mom gave him her undivided attention. That was hard to watch. I also noticed that I hadn't heard from Elly in days. She had left me messages almost daily until I confronted Eric. He must've said something to her.

Tonight we were having a family dinner, and Mom invited him. Lisa was also coming, and, unfortunately, I couldn't consume wine because of my prescription; otherwise, I would've had a chilled bottle right next to my plate. The good news was that my niece, Olivia, would be here too, and I was looking forward to that.

Dad and I were watching a Knicks game, his favorite team—well, now he loved the Nets too, since they'd moved to Brooklyn. When they built the Barclays Center, he was stoked, especially since it was walking distance from the house. I got him season Nets tickets for his last birthday and became his favorite daughter. Just kidding. *I am always his favorite!* And being the music lover that I am, I'd seen tons of concerts at Barclays too, most with my Aunt Janet who was also a music lover—John Mayer, Pink, Justin Timberlake, Paul McCartney, Lionel Richie, Bruno Mars, Alicia Keys, Coldplay, The Rolling Stones with Mary J. Blige, Barbra Streisand and, of course, Beyoncé and Jay Z. I was supposed to see Billy Joel for New Year's Eve but was in the hospital then. If I wasn't shopping for shoes, I was somewhere enjoying live music.

Mom walked into the living room and said, "Guess who just called?"

"Who?" Dad asked, eyes on the screen.

"Not for you," she replied.

"For me?" I asked.

"Yeah. Christina called," she said. I had to maintain a blank expression, though I was happy and curious.

"Which one is Christina again?" Dad asked.

"That's Bailey's co-worker," Mom said. "She's coming to see you."

"She is?" I asked. I wanted to see Christina but not here.

"Yeah, she said she's tried to call you and call the hospital, but she hasn't heard from you. She didn't know where you were, so she tried us."

"Oh, okay. Um, when is she coming?"

"She'll be here in about an hour."

"You should've told Bailey first," Dad said.

"What? I thought it'd be nice for her to see Christina," she said. "You too are really close, Bailey. It'll be good for your memory."

"No, that's fine. I'll go freshen up," I said and left the living room—then I stopped to ask Mom, "What did you tell Christina?"

"Tell her? Nothing."

She told her something. I needed to figure out what that was somehow before Christina got here. Then I heard her tell Dad, "I'm surprised we haven't seen Elly." *Ugh. The mention of her name made my hand form a fist.*

I heard the doorbell and headed back downstairs. My parents were talking to Christina in the foyer.

"Bailey!" Christina said and hugged me tight. I reluctantly patted her back.

"Hi. Christina."

"Hi. You look great."

"Thanks," I said while my parents stared. "Hey, let's go for a walk." I grabbed my coat off the coat rack and opened the door. My parents were going to either sit right next to us or be in another room listening in on us. It was best to just leave.

"Okay," Christina said. "So how have you been? I had no idea where you were, or how you were doing." Christina was a true New Yorker—direct, talked fast, sarcastic, no patience. *I wish I could be more direct.* She was about my height, five foot seven, and she had the body of a teenage boy, which she liked having. She and her husband were avid runners, health nuts, and had two sweet little girls.

"I've been fine," I said looking back. I wanted to see if either of my parents was there standing on the front stoop. They weren't.

"Yeah?" Christina asked while looking at me sideways. "And you're coming back to work on Monday?"

"Yeah. What did my mother tell you?"

"Nothing really. Just that you've been out of the hospital and have been staying with them for some days. She also said it'd be good for your memories or your memory—I don't know. What's she talking about?"

We turned the corner, and I gave Christina a big hug. It was obvious she was confused by her reluctant back pat.

"I'm sorry. I know you have questions."

"Uh, yeah. What's up with the delayed response?"

"Let's get some coffee, and I'll catch you up."

"Let's do it."

We sat with our coffees, and I took several sips of my caramel latte.

"Uh, hello?" Christina said.

"Sorry. Man, where do I start?"

"The accident—I heard it was a car accident, and then you were in a coma?"

"Yes, that's true. I actually still don't know the details of the accident to tell you the truth. My parents didn't want to discuss it and there was so much else going on anyway."

"Like what? How long were you in the hospital?"

"I was in a coma for a week, and then they kept me a few more days for observation. And then I was home."

"Oh. Okay. Why are you at your parent's place now?" I didn't want to get into the Eric issue. I wasn't ready to deal with it, and Christina wouldn't respect me if I told her I was going to stay with him. I didn't know if I was going to or not, but it was best to keep it all to myself for now.

"Um, well … my family thinks I have amnesia."

"Amnesia? Why do they think that?"

"I may have led them to believe that when I woke up from my coma."

She paused, and then cackled hysterically.

I hadn't planned on telling Christina, but once I saw her, I couldn't lie *to her*. I needed someone in my corner, and she was the one.

"You are a nut job! So they're all tip-toeing around thinking you don't remember anything?"

"Not exactly. Things are *kind of* back to normal. Actually, they're better. My mother has been kind to me, cooking for me, and spending time with me."

"What? Not, Mrs. Pierce the Eric-lover." *Even she knows.*

"Yeah, she has. It's been really nice. I mean it's a complete one-eighty. She doesn't dismiss me, and she brought me mac and cheese at the hospital—"

"Mac and cheese! That's reason enough to fake amnesia."

"Ha ha." She understood my infatuation with the yellow carb.

"What about your sisters? Don't tell me they've come around too?"

"No, they haven't."

"Damn. Wow, this is crazy. Okay, so what is your plan? Are you going to wake up one day and say you remember everything?"

"I actually didn't think that part through when I was in the hospital. But you know my family. We've mastered ignoring pink elephants, so I figured my amnesia would eventually be one of those things that were treated like it didn't exist, especially since I *know* everyone now."

"Okay."

"Like when my sister Tina gained a lot of weight in high school, stopped needing tampons, then lost her boyfriend and the weight. Or when my Uncle Donnie died and then Aunt Janet spent months *away* – in alcohol rehab – before moving in with my parents. We're a family who *overlooks* and moves on. Addressing issues is what *other families* do, which is why I was so surprised when my parents wanted me to go to therapy."

"You freaked them out. Even *they* don't know what to do with amnesia. How's therapy going?"

"I kind of botched the first session. But I have a new therapist I'll be seeing soon."

"But what are you going to do at therapy with fake amnesia?"

"Everyone can use a little therapy."

"Does anyone else think you have amnesia? Work?"

"No. No one else."

"This is … a damn reality show. You need to call Seacrest." We both laughed.

As much as Christina wanted to stay for dinner and witness the *reality show*, she had to get home to her own family. Everyone was at my parent's house, and Olivia was showing me some photos of her friends.

"Are you going to print any of these?" I asked.

"That's so old school, Aunt B," Olivia said.

"What if you lose your phone?"

"I'll still have everything on the cloud." *Of course.*

"Dinner is ready," Aunt Janet called from the kitchen.

I whispered to Olivia, "Sit next to me, okay?"

"Okay."

Everyone entered the dining room, and Olivia sat next to me as planned. Eric was standing, and the only remaining seat was next to Dad.

"Olivia, sit over there, so Uncle Eric can sit next to Aunt Bailey and me," Mom said. *Ugh.*

"Great," Eric said, smiling.

"This is nice," Mom said and patted Eric's hand. Then Dad said grace, and we dug in.

"The casserole looks good, Lisa," I said.

"Thanks," she said without even glancing my way. "What did you make?" she asked me. *Oh brother.*

"I didn't make anything, but I picked up dessert. Peach cobbler." *Since she loves peach cobbler.*

"I don't eat that anymore," she said. *Of course you don't.* "Doesn't the Bible say that if a person doesn't cook, he doesn't eat?"

"When's the last time you were in anybody's church?" Dad asked her. We all snickered, but she only focused on *mine* and cut her eyes at me.

"It's actually: if a man will not work he shouldn't eat," Mom said.

"Oh. So, how's work, Lisa?" Eric asked. Everyone chuckled again. She was currently *between jobs*.

"Well, Bailey hasn't been to work either," Lisa said.

"Yeah, but she has a job to go to," Dad said. *I wish he hadn't.* He was frustrated about loaning her money and her fluctuating occupations: hairdresser, caterer, web designer, *exotic dancer*—Dad didn't know about that one. My brother Chuck used to tell me everything.

"Whatever," said Lisa.

"Anyway, how's your research project coming along Eric?" Mom asked.

"It's good. Making steady gains," he said. *He talks with food in his mouth. It drives me crazy.* "I'm actually being honored next week by an organization called FIP. I was hoping you'd join me, Bails. Black tie, live music—it's a pretty big deal." *What is he doing?*

"I'm not really up for it," I said.

"What do you mean? It sounds nice. And they're recognizing your husband. You should be there," Mom said.

"Karen," Dad said to her.

"What? Why wouldn't she go?" Mom asked.

"I'm just not up to it, that's all," I said.

"But you're up to going back to work? Be nice. Get dressed up and go with him."

"Karen." Dad said.

"We'll see," I said and cut my eyes at Eric.

My sister watched me. She had a smirk, realizing that something had been going on with Eric and me. *Trouble in paradise,* and she loved it. I ate the rest of my dinner quietly while everyone else talked. I'd been headache-free for days and didn't want to bring one on. Then Lisa served herself a piece of the peach cobbler.

Bitch.

BACK TO THE GRIND

Monday morning I got up super early for work. I looked forward to being away from the family. Christina said that she'd meet me in the lobby at nine, but I couldn't wait until then. Plus I thought it might be better to be there before everyone versus making an entrance.

I arranged for a car service to pick me up, and I took the ride from Brooklyn to midtown Manhattan. I got to work at seven, which was pretty much earlier than anyone got in, with the exception of the receptionist and an admin or two.

I walked into my office, and it was almost as I left it. My assistant, Carrie, must have straightened up for me because all of the folders were in order, and my desk was neat, which had never been the case.

Christina worked in product development but was aware of what went on in all departments, so she'd brought me up-to-date the day before. I sat at my desk and caught up on several emails, and then I went through my files to see what the updates were with a few of my clients.

I heard footsteps outside my door; it was already after eight o'clock. Christina and Carrie were in the doorway with flowers and balloons. I was happy to see them.

"Good morning!" said Carrie and hugged me. "I'm so glad you're back."

"Me too," said Christina.

"It's good to be back," I said. Several other people stopped by to greet me as well.

"I'll leave you two alone," Carrie said and left.

"So how are things for the *Real Housewife of Disremember*?" Christina asked.

"Oh be quiet."

"Oh! We have a meeting in two minutes. Come on."

I grabbed my tablet and followed her to our main conference room. On our way there, everyone we came in contact with stopped and greeted me. It was great and much better than dinner with Lisa and Eric. By the time we finally made it to the conference room, ten minutes late, everyone was in a deep discussion about something. When they noticed me, they stopped and clapped. It was sweet. Then Tommy said, "I knew you were off at fat camp! You look great—welcome back!" They caught me up and we had our meeting.

Time was flying by, and I felt useful and productive. *Being a taste-tester for my parents and learning sitcom theme songs could be considered useful too, though.* My boss, Dennis popped in my office.

"Look at you!" said Dennis. He was a tall, loud, extrovert who filled every room he entered.

"Hi, Dennis." He embraced me a little too long and almost *missed* my cheek with his lips. It was my own fault. I'd joined his team back when I used my *pretty* to get ahead. I'd been attempting to get him to see my real talents for the past year.

"It's great to have you back. How's your first day going?"

"Good. I didn't realize how much I missed this place."

"And you're back full-time?"

"I think so, but I'll play it by ear."

"Sounds good. Hey, let's grab a bite this week. Put something on my calendar," he said and rubbed my arm.

"Will do." *Can we dine in the human resources office?*

Christina came by a few minutes later. "How's it going?" she asked.

"Great. I'm glad I didn't wait any longer to come back to work."

"Me too. What are you doing for lunch?"

"Aren't you taking me to lunch?" I joked.

"Of course I am! How about Thai?"

"That sounds perfect. Ready now?"

"Let's do it."

I grabbed my coat from behind the door.

"*What* color is that thing? And where on Earth did you get it?"

"It's *chartreuse,* and I got it at Bloomies. I saw it on a mannequin and thought, you know what I need?"

"A mirror?"

I hit her arm.

"Let's go *Anna Wintour.*"

"Who?"

"Exactly."

As we walked down the busy Manhattan sidewalk, I almost broke a sweat trying to keep up with Christina's pace. She didn't wear heels, and I did. *I also didn't bench press a thousand or run alongside trains for sport.* Kidding, but she was no joke. I was so glad when we arrived at the restaurant.

"You won," I said, out of breath.

"What?"

"How do you always manage to navigate through millions of people at fifty miles per hour?"

"Aw, you're tired. You've just been out of the office and out of practice. Buck up," she said. "Table for two please."

"There's a twenty-minute wait," said the hostess.

"Bar?" asked Christina.

"Sure," I said.

"So, have you spoken to Bryce?" asked Christina. Bryce was a good mutual friend and former colleague who was the corporate counsel at knirD woN before starting his own law practice. We were like the Three Musketeers and had remained close.

"No, how is he?"

"He's good. He said that he visited you in the hospital, but couldn't handle seeing you in a coma."

"Yeah, he's not good with that kind of stuff."

"He asked me to let him know when it was *safe* to call you," she said and chuckled.

"What's funny?"

"You're going to have to explain to him your fake amnesia situation."

"First of all, it's *faux-nesia*, and how does he know about it?"

"After I spoke to your mom, before I visited you, I spoke to him. We were both trying to figure out what your mom meant by your *current condition* and *help you remember*."

"Oh, brother. I'll reach out to him later. I'm glad the rest of my family doesn't know … anyone I know."

"True. Okay, guess time. Who's pregnant, getting married, and sleeping with Diane?"

"I'm assuming that these aren't all the same person?"

She tilted her head. "No."

Christina was one of the most ambitious and respected women at the company—and she *always* knew the latest gossip. People just told her things.

"Let me see … Getting married—Lucy?"

"Yes!"

"Sleeping with Diane … Please don't say Dennis."

"No, but you're close."

"Okay, I don't even know what that means. Um … Billiam?"

"Yes!"

"Ew!"

"Well …"

"And pregnant. I don't know; that could be anyone."

"Who would we be super happy for?"

"Ooh—Rachel?"

"Yes!"

"Yay!" Rachel was a colleague of ours who was forty and had tried to have a baby for over eight years. "That is awesome. How far along is she?"

"Five months. In the safe zone."

"Nice.

"Orders, ladies," said the bartender.

"I'll do the basil fish with the veggies. No rice or potato. And a green tea," said Christina.

"I'll have the same but fry my fish and put it in a bun. Do the same with my potatoes please. And a bottled water."

"Ha. Got it," said the bartender.

"Hey, I guessed three out of three so you're paying for lunch right?" I asked Christina.

"I had to help you with the third one."

"Okay, let's talk about work and expense it."

"We did. Rachel is pregnant."

"True. Cheers."

"Cheers." We clicked water glasses.

"Actually," I said. "I do have a work item to discuss."

"Shoot."

"It's kind of a new year's resolution too. I want to go for that senior manager slot, but Dennis is a roadblock. He doesn't take me seriously, so I need to get the attention of someone else who can help make that happen."

"Hmm ... I heard about some big West Coast project that's coming up. It's a collaboration between marketing and product development."

"Where'd you hear about it?"

"Stephen."

"Ugh."

"I know." Stephen was the thorn in my flesh at knirD. I usually got along with everyone, but he was such a misogynist jerk. He was a creative marketing guy, which was why he hadn't been terminated yet, given all the complaints brought against him. He reported to Dennis too.

"Who else can I ask about it besides him or Dennis?"

"I'll find out. It's still in the works so you have some time."

"Okay. How are things with your promotion to director?"

"It's looking great, actually. I just need to stay out of trouble until review time next quarter, and it's a done deal." She was kidding; she never got into trouble.

"That's awesome, Christina! You deserve it."

"Thanks a bunch Bailey."

She was my inspiration. This year we were both going to get promoted.

When I got back to my parent's house that night, I was excited to share how work was when I saw Mom and Eric on the sofa.

"Hi," they said to me in unison, as two people who'd spent too much time together.

"Hi—" I said but Mom had already turned around to continue talking with Eric. *She's reverting.* I stood there for a moment feeling disregarded then headed to the kitchen.

"How was work?" Dad asked. *I can always count on him.*

"It was great." I filled him and my Aunt Janet in on my day. Well, it was the modified version of how someone with amnesia would return to work—reading files, shadowing people, asking questions, etc.

Eric walked in holding a navy cocktail dress on a hanger with my mother all cheery behind him. I looked at the dress and then at him.

"What's this?" I asked.

"No pressure but in case you decide to join me at the ceremony this Friday, I got you something to wear," he said.

"Isn't that so sweet?" Mom said. I hated when he did stuff like this, especially in front of my parents. If I reacted the way I felt, angrily, Mom would think I was an ungrateful brat or still somehow confused about things.

"It's pretty. Thanks," I said, then took the dress and went upstairs. I knew Mom must've thought that I was being difficult. *Maybe I should give Eric a hug or something, so she sees I'm trying.*

There was a knock on my door. *Eric.*

"Come in."

"Hey." He sat next to me, and I stood up. "I didn't mean to upset you, Bailey. I just wanted to get you something nice. Really." *I didn't respond.* "You need time. I get it. I'm going to give you space. I can see that my coming by is bothering you. I'll stay away. I just hope you come home soon ... I need you. We can make this work ... I'll do whatever you need me to do, sweetie. Please." He stood up to leave. Before he closed the door behind him, he said, "I love you."

I sat back on the bed as a tear rolled down my face. *Why do I end up being the one feeling guilty?*

HERE WE GO AGAIN

A few nights later, I'd been preparing dinner with Aunt Janet. We had music playing and weren't saying much when Mom walked in.

"Have either of you heard from Eric?" Mom asked.

"I haven't," I said. And my aunt shook her head.

"He hasn't been by or called. Do you think he's joining us for dinner tonight?"

"I don't know, Mom, but I don't think so."

She nodded slowly then said, "You know, it's not easy for a husband to bounce back after his wife's been in a serious accident, coma, and then has amnesia."

"Mom."

"Let me finish. He's trying, Bailey. We all are. Why are you pushing him away?"

"I'm not pushing him away."

"Then why are you here instead of at home with your husband?" *Ouch.*

"Karen!" Aunt Janet said.

"Do you want me to leave, Mom?"

Shadé Akande

"I just wonder if we've enabled you," she said.

"She doesn't want you to leave, Bailey. Tell her that you don't want her to leave, Karen," said Aunt Janet.

"If being here is impacting your relationship with your husband, then you should be with your husband," said Mom.

"Fine." I went upstairs, called a taxi, and stuffed all of my things in my overnight bags. I kissed my aunt and mother, and left.

"Where to?" said the taxi driver.

"Trump SoHo, please."

The next evening, I realized all of my clothes needed laundering, and I wouldn't be able to request that until the morning. I thought about going shopping for some basics but was actually not in the mood. *Not in the mood to shop – that's serious, and a first.* I wanted to spend the weekend in bed ordering room service, so clean clothes were a requirement. I decided to go home and pick up some items since Eric was at his awards ceremony.

When I keyed into the apartment, I was surprised to see Eric on the sofa in his tuxedo with a glass of wine. He stood up.

"Bails."

"What are you doing here? Why aren't you at your event?"

"I couldn't go without you."

"What?"

"I just can't—" *Is he crying?*

"Eric?"

He kneeled down in front of me and put his face on my stomach, holding my waist. *I can't deal with this right now. I feel so alone. I don't know what to believe anymore.* He kissed my stomach, then my chest, and then my neck …

Don't be stupid, Bailey. Don't be stupid, Bailey … Don't be stupid, Bailey … ~~Don't be~~ stupid Bailey … We were kissing.

I had no idea where my clothes were and was not sure which room I was in. I was wearing just one sock, though I hadn't started the previous evening wearing any socks. The clock said seven, and I was assuming that was a.m., but there was no way to really know because the blinds were closed, and I just had a night of sex … with Eric.

Was this all a dream? Am I about to wake up in my hotel room fully clothed?

"Good morning," Eric said as he turned over and held me.

"Hi." *What have I done?*

A few minutes later Eric dozed off, so I grabbed a robe and put on a pot of coffee. I poured a cup and leaned against the kitchen island in a daze. I went to pour another cup and realized that I'd already emptied the coffee pot. *How many cups did I just drink?* I got a bowl of cereal and sat at the dining room table. *I forgot the milk?* I ate one Honey Nut O at a time.

Eric entered the dining room fully dressed and shaven. He kissed me on the forehead.

"I—"

"Sorry sweetie. I've got to run. I need to get to the lab. I'll see you tonight!" And he was gone. Did he really have to leave or was he avoiding the situation?

After a warm bath, I spent hours shopping online while watching TV and playing music. I needed the multiple stimuli to distract my thoughts. I was disappointed in myself; I felt stupid—*and* free. Stupid of course for letting Eric back in. But also free because, while in the hotel room, I felt homeless and unwanted. I wanted to be at my parents but not if my mother didn't want me there and it caused our relationship to regress. My phone rang. *Mother.*

"Hi, Mom."

"How are you?"

"Fine. How are you?"

"I'm doing fine. I spoke to Eric and he sounded so happy." *Sigh.*

"Yeah ..."

"I wanted to say that I'm sorry if I came down too hard on you the other day," she said. *What? I looked at my phone.* "I just want you to be okay. No—happy. I'm glad that you're working things out with Eric."

"Thanks, Mom."

"Hey, let's have lunch next weekend at S'Mac."

"Yeah?" *S'Mac is only the best macaroni and cheese exclusive restaurant on the planet!*

"Yeah, and then we can go window shopping."

"Okay, Mom, explain this *window shopping* to me. You go to stores, but you *don't* purchase anything? Are the stores not open? Do they not take US currency—what's the deal?"

She laughed and said, "Okay, we'll *shop.*"

"Now *that* I understand."

"I'll talk to you soon."

"Okay. Say hi to Dad and Aunt Janet for me."

"I will."

I felt happy. *I've got my mother back ... with a side of Eric.*

I went into our den and reviewed several of our bills in the file cabinet that I never touch. I had no idea what our current mortgage or other household bills were—Eric took care of everything. Once I saw how much it actually cost to live our life, I knew that I couldn't afford it by myself. I started to have even more second thoughts about a divorce ...

ACT L

I was back at work after seeing Eric a total of twenty minutes the entire weekend. On Sunday, I awoke to a dozen roses on the nightstand with a note that said, "Off to the lab again. Enjoy your day. Love, Eric." He didn't get home until midnight as he had the night before. And when I left in the morning, he was knocked out. He must've thought that he could avoid me until I, what—*forgot I was mad at him*? Actually ... that had worked on me many times before for less serious crimes. I didn't necessarily forget then, just too much time had passed to bring anything up. I have my mom back, and it's almost worth it to just forgive Eric. He was more apologetic than he'd ever been our entire marriage. And the tears—that had to mean something ... right?

No. We had to at least discuss it if we were going to have a chance. But I needed to focus on work right now. That West Coast project had my name all over it, and it was time to be serious about something and propel my career. I wanted to be the ambitious, sharp person I once was in my youth.

Christina was a gem and helped me get all of the information I needed from Pierre, a VP who was also one of Dennis's peers. And I'd spent the morning doing research and getting the additional answers I needed. I was ready. I just needed to get all my *other responsibilities* completed first. It was lunchtime, but I was on a roll. I couldn't stop now.

Carrie peeked in and said, "You have a call on line two from Sinai Women's Center."

"Okay. Would you mind grabbing me a salad when you go out?"

"Sure."

"Thanks," I said and picked up my phone. "Bailey Bryant."

"Hi, Mrs. Bryant. I'm calling because you missed your scheduled neurology appointment last Friday with Dr. Harrison," said the appointment clerk.

"Shoot. I'm sorry, I totally forgot about it."

"I understand. In order to maintain clearance to be back at work, we'd need to see you this week for routine scans, just to ensure that everything is still okay."

I couldn't let anything get in the way of my being cleared to work now. I finally had career aspirations. "Of course. Um, do you have anything available for tomorrow morning?"

"The next available appointment we have is for Thursday at eight a.m."

"Okay, I'll take it. I'm putting it in my calendar right now and will definitely be there."

"Great. I've got you down."

"Oh, and I went to the pharmacy for a refill, but they needed my doctor to send in authorization. Can you ask Dr. Harrison to do that, please?"

"Unfortunately, the doctor won't be able to authorize any additional refills until she sees you. Are you having bad headaches?"

"No, I've been okay. It can wait until Thursday."

"Okay."

A few hours later, Dennis popped into my office. "Got a second?" he asked.

"Sure, come on in."

"I hear that you had a meeting with Pierre."

"Yeah, I had some questions about the upcoming LA project."

"Oh. Okay. Why would you be interested in that?" *How condescending.*

"I think the projects that I've managed so far are right in line with this one, just on a larger scale. And I'm very much interested in it."

"Hmm. Well, why didn't you just ask me about it?"

"Dennis, you just asked me why *I* was interested in the project. Obviously, you didn't think —"

"No, it's just that … you just got back and, well, you've never mentioned wanting to take on more work in the past. That's all." *Yeah, right.*

"Well, I planned to speak with you about it after I learned all the details, which I have and … Dennis, I want you to consider me to spearhead it."

"There's a lot of research to be conducted —"

"I have an outline on how best to approach that right here with some preliminary research already conducted." I handed him a folder. He skimmed it, looked up at me, and then read through the rest.

"There's going to be a lot of travel."

"To snow-free California? Sign me up."

He was quiet. "This is not only for our new beverage, but we're also re-launching—"

"BerryLish? I know. Here are some pilot mock-ups of the bottle packaging from the graphics team." I handed him another folder.

"How'd you get these?"

"They actually like me, Dennis." *He knew what I meant.* No one liked his golden boy, Stephen. I was feeling pretty good. I had answers for all of his objections. I was not taking no for an answer.

"I have to be honest. This is ... impressive." *Yay!*

"Thank you."

"But I don't think you're ready yet," he said and stood up.

Damn. Think fast Bailey, think ..."Have you secured a spokesperson for the new beverage?" I asked.

"No. Why?"

Just like my hospital opportunity when I instantly thought to say I didn't recognize anyone in the room, this was another *ACTL* moment—*A Chance to Lie.* I needed this project, the way I needed to no longer be insignificant to my family. Pepsi had Beyoncé, Coke had Taylor Swift, and knirD needed someone big too.

"I know … Gwen Stefani. And I have a good inclination that she'd be interested."

Dennis turned around. *I don't know Gwen Stefani.* "Really? And what makes you think she'd be interested?"

"I can't disclose those details."

He looked at me for a minute. "I'll tell you what. There's a meeting tomorrow with the products team at two o'clock. You should join us," he said. "I'd like to introduce them to the new project manager."

"Really? I've got it?"

"Can you get us Stefani?"

"I can *get* you Stefani." It just may not be *Gwen* Stefani …

"Then you've got it." He shook my hand and headed for the door.

"Thank you, Dennis. You won't be sorry."

"I better not be."

"See, I'm not just a pretty face."

"Who said you were pretty?" he joked.

"Well, *beautiful* would've sounded conceited, don't you think?"

He chuckled and turned to leave before saying, "Hey, let's keep the Stefani thing between us, okay?"

"Of course."

Then he left. *I was stoked!* Not thinking of the Gwen piece, of course. And I loved this feeling. It brought back memories of winning spelling bees, chess tournaments and being fifth-grade salutatorian. Why'd I trade all that in to be a jolly cheerleader and participate in pageants? I felt like washing the makeup off my face and throwing my heels in the trash —

but not *these* heels, that would be wasteful. I had already spent the money, *right*?

I called Christina to tell her the news, and she screamed through the phone. *I left out the Stefani part.* It looked as though I'd be having a lot of late nights in the office. Eric had been avoiding home anyway, so it didn't matter. I'd deactivated my Facebook account due to the *faux-nesia* since I was "friends" with family members and that would've been a challenge. But I got on there, and searched through who I knew who could've possibly known Gwen Stefani or her manager or publicist. I sent out two hundred messages and crossed my fingers. A few hours later, over one hundred "Sorry, can't help" replies. The best approach would've been to ask a few clients and colleagues, but that may have gotten back to Dennis.

I headed to the elevator after putting in a twelve-hour day and saw Christina there.

"Have you checked your email recently?" she asked.

"No, what's up?"

"Check it."

I pulled out my phone and read an email from Dennis. "Are you kidding me?"

"He didn't mention this when you two spoke?" she asked.

"No, I would've told you. Ugh. What the hell?"

An email had gone out from Dennis, with an outline for tomorrow's LA project meeting introducing the project managers—yes, *plural*. Bailey Bryant *and* Stephen Murray. *Stephen freakin' Murray, my adversary.* So not only was I *not* spearheading this alone and showcasing my strengths to get promoted, but I also had to work closely with a man who made me want to curse — *sons of bitches! See?*

THURSDAY

I had hoped that having an early doctor's appointment would decrease the amount of time I'd have to actually sit in the doctor's office. I'd arrived here at seven thirty for an eight o'clock appointment, and it was almost nine. If I hadn't needed the prescription for my headaches, I would have left. Actually, I didn't think I needed it. Aspirin had been working just fine. *They've taken my scans, my blood pressure, and I've peed in a cup; let me just leave and go to work.*

"Good morning," Dr. Harrison said and closed the door.

"Is it still morning?" I sat back down.

"I know. I know it took a little while. But right when I was wrapping up one thing and about to write your prescription, I learned that I can't."

I waited all this time, and she's not going to write my prescription? "Why—" I attempted to ask.

She raised her hand and said, "Everything is okay. Your scans look great, and there are no red flags."

"So?"

"Your pregnancy is going to prevent you from taking any prescribed medications at this time." She beamed.

"My pregnancy?" I sat up straight.

"Your pregnancy."

"Oh my God."

"Yes, you're definitely in the very early stages. I'm glad you came in, and I'm glad that your prescription ended when it did. What have you been taking in its place?"

"Just some aspirin and not all the time. The headaches aren't nearly as bad as they were a week ago. Wait, I'm pregnant. And you're sure?"

"I am sure. I'm assuming this wasn't planned?"

Oh, yeah, she knows about Eric. "No, I can't say that it was. I forgot about birth control. Whatever I was using before the accident must've … ended."

"What were you using? Oh, you probably don't remember that," she said. I shrugged. *In that moment, I actually didn't remember.* "How are you feeling?"

"Surprised. Um … but this is a blessing, right?"

"Yes, it is. It's your first right?"

"Yes … So, Dr. Harrison, tell me what to do now — and what not to do. What I shouldn't eat — everything."

"I can give you some general information, but you'd of course want to make an appointment with your OB/GYN."

"Right, I'll do that. Do you know who that is?"

"Yes, it's here in your file. Here you go," she said and wrote down my gynecologist's contact information. "And I want to see you back in a month. I'll work with your gynecologist on any precautions we'd need to take with your amnesia."

"Yes … of course."

She then walked me through what I should expect during the first trimester, then I left her office overwhelmed and with a lot of brochures. *I'm going to be a mother.* I wanted to call someone, but there was no one I was ready to tell. In a flash, I thought about the situation with Eric, my new work project, my mother. *I just needed to get to work.* Then I thought of something and went back to the doctor.

"Dr. Harrison?"

"Yes. Is everything okay?"

"Yeah, fine. Uhh, do you know anyone who may know Gwen Stefani?" I hadn't had any Facebook luck and Dennis was already bugging me. *I'm not crazy ...*

"Um ... no," she said.

"Okay then. Bye." And I left.

SECRETS

The weekend came, and I was ready to burst because I hadn't yet told anyone I was pregnant. It was still early, but keeping something this big to myself was hard, especially since I'd been hiding major truths already these past couple of months. I was afraid of bringing on head pains, especially since I could no longer take my prescription. I had lunch and great macaroni with Mom and was tempted to tell her a few times, especially when she held my arm as we walked down the street. Then I met up with Christina afterward and wanted to tell her too.

"I can't believe you have me in this boutique. These prices are outrageous," Christina said. "Two hundred and fifty dollars for shoes that ruin your back?"

"That's not bad. Look at these, four hundred dollars."

"Please don't tell me that you're buying those?"

"Nooo … That'd be crazy—since I already have them."

"Bailey! Can I give *you* a new year's resolution?"

"I'm pretty sure it doesn't work that way."

"Four hundred?"

"Did you *just* meet me? Hi, I'm Bailey Bryant, and shoes are my sustenance."

"Right. Couldn't you have taken me to another shoe store? I just need a pair of shoes for my husband's birthday dinner. Let's go somewhere that sells less-expensive shoes."

"They have places like that?" I asked.

She rolled her eyes.

"Bryce is going to the dinner, right?"

"Yep, he'll be there."

"How about these, Christina? The heel isn't too high, and they're only a hundred and seventy dollars."

"I love how you say *only*. They're actually not bad."

"Can she see these in an eight please?" I asked the saleslady. She nodded and headed to the back.

"Okay, if I get them, can we go?" asked Christina.

"*Go?* You have to get a matching clutch and a necklace."

"What? That's a damn pyramid scheme. I only told you to help me with shoes not the add-ons."

"You've got to get them."

"Do I have to bring in ten people next week too?"

"No, I've already done that. Wait, didn't you just spend two hundred dollars on running shoes?"

"Not the same. Those running shoes had a three-tier interlocking reinforcement that—"

"Snore! Are they pretty and do they falsify your height? That's all that matters."

She chuckled and said, "Why do I bother?"

"I should actually get a pair of these flats myself."

"Did I just hear you right? Flats? Are they a gift?"

"No, just for when I might need extra comfort or something."

"I never thought I'd see the day that you'd wear flats, if you were pregnant or broke a leg maybe."

I should tell her. I want to tell her. Ugh! I need to tell her. I won't tell her yet. "I know right. Hey, Crystal Snow concert tickets went on sale today."

"Who?"

"Cryst—Never mind. I forgot whom I was talking to. What do you listen to when you go running?"

"I listen to audio books or just my thoughts."

"Instead of great banging beats? I never understood how you didn't love music."

"Just like I don't understand four-hundred-dollar shoes."

"Ahh, *touché*."

When I walked into my apartment, Eric was on the sofa, on his cell phone. He waved at me.

"Yes, of course. That was my conclusion as well … Okay, well we're on the right track then … Sounds good … We'll try that approach on Monday … Great … Bye," he said and hung up.

"Hey, stranger," I said.

"Hey," he said and stood up. "I was just about to head to—"

"Have a seat, Eric. I know you've been avoiding me."

"No, it's just been a crazy week that's all." I tilted my head. "We need to talk." *Every man's favorite sentence.*

"Um, sure. But can we do it later. I really was—"

"I'm pregnant."

"You're pregnant?"

I nodded.

Eric knelt down and held me with his face on my stomach. He tried to kiss me, and I held his face.

"Eric."

"Yes?"

I patted the sofa and he sat.

"We have a lot to discuss."

"What, Bails. We're having a baby. It's great! Look, I admit that you weren't happy with me recently …" *What kind of admittance is that?* "But I'm going to do anything and everything to make you happy. I promise. I love you, and it's all about you, this baby, and our growing family now. I mean it. Whatever you need, just tell me. I'm ready to do anything. Anything. And I'm truly sorry for any pain that I may have caused you, and I want to spend the rest of my life waking up next to you. Okay?"

Sigh. "Okay."

Eric and I spent the next hour talking about the baby on the way. And he was already looking at me differently. It was like this new sparkle in his eye for me, and he couldn't stop touching my belly, even though there were, of course, no visible signs that I was pregnant yet. I was hopeful. *I needed to be.* I needed peace and … *easy.* There was too much on my plate now, and I definitely didn't want to be a single mother. And, well, he *did* apologize. He also promised to be home every night by six o'clock and make me a healthy dinner or pick up a healthy dinner. I agreed not to work late more than one night a week too. Things were looking up.

Eric had to head to New Jersey to meet with his client at the lab, so he reluctantly left the apartment.

Later that night, I cooked a healthy seafood dinner the way I used to, and Eric and I were all baby talk. We decided not to tell anyone until I got to my second trimester. Outside of Christina, I didn't want anyone at work to know anyway because of the LA project. Knowledge of my pregnancy would cause Dennis to think my productivity would be limited. *It's a shame, but it's true.* I wanted to tell Olivia, though. It was going to be hard keeping it from her.

"Should we think of baby names now, or wait until we meet him first?" Eric asked.

"Him? What makes you think the baby's a boy?"

"It has to be. The first one's a boy, and then next year —"

"Next year?"

He smiled and said, "Yes, next year we can have a beautiful little girl." Then he added, "She'll look just like you."

"Don't even try it," I said and hit his arm. "This, right here is a girl."

"Hear me out," he continued. "This one will be a boy, and he'll grow up to love and protect his mother well into her old age. And then he can also protect his little sister from horny boys."

"Um hmm. We'll call that plan B."

Eric rubbed my belly.

We're going to be okay.

GETTING BURNED

A few weeks later, my parents and Aunt Janet went to visit my brother, Stewart, and his family in Pasadena for a week. I had brunch with them the day they flew out. Lisa stopped by too, and I thought it was sweet of her until I saw the bag of laundry in her hand. She hadn't even remembered that it was the day of their trip. When she saw their luggage by the door, it hit her. She didn't join us but instead grabbed a few pieces of bacon then headed down the hall to bust some suds.

After we all ate, my parents and aunt decided to head out to the airport early in case there was traffic or the security lines were long.

"Lisa, don't forget to lock up when you go," Dad said.

"I'll be sure to lock up. Have a great trip," she said and hugged them all before heading back to the laundry room.

Olivia and I saw them all off then watched some TV while I waited for Eric to pick me up. We were an hour into a really good movie when he arrived.

"Could we leave in thirty minutes? I just want to see what happens to the girl's boyfriend," I asked him.

"Sure, no problem," Eric said and headed toward the kitchen. He got to the hallway and said, "Do you smell that?"

"Smell what?" I said. When he didn't reply, Olivia and I looked at each other and went to see what he was talking about. Near the top of the stairs leading to the basement, we smelled smoke. Then Lisa came out of the laundry room, and her expression was identical to ours. Eric headed down to the basement and we weren't far behind.

"Stay up here, Olivia," I said.

"Oh my God—it's coming from in here!" he said. Then Lisa ran down the stairs too. There was smoke coming from under the door to my Aunt Janet's room. She kept it locked, so I ran in the other direction, toward the second floor. My mom kept a spare key in her bedroom but … *how would I explain that I had remembered that?* She kept the key in the closet in a container that had a combination lock—I knew all of this because of all the errands I ran for her throughout the years, but I couldn't explain knowing that now. I stood halfway up the stairwell frozen. I heard Eric below pounding against the door and coughing. The smoke had begun to make its way toward the kitchen. *What do I do? I couldn't move.*

"Aunt B! What are you doing?" Olivia asked me with a phone in her hand.

I needed to get that key … But—

"Aunt B, let's go!" Olivia pulled me down the stairs and outside to the front of the house. "I called the fire department," she said. Then Lisa and Eric ran out of the house and were coughing. I just stared at the house, immobile and heard the fire truck coming up the street.

I'm a terrible person.

The firemen put out the fire before it caused any damage to the other floors, but the entire basement was ruined. They said the fire was caused by candles that were still lit and either fell over or something fell on them. *Damn Aunt Janet and her candles.* We were all checked for smoke inhalation but were fine since we'd gotten out in time.

I walked through the ashes of what remained in the basement. There was hardly anything recognizable. All her nice furniture, photo frames, closet full of clothes, sentimental items from her late husband, art—it was all destroyed.

"Man, I can't even tell what this was," said Eric with a drenched, black object in his hand.

"Or this," said Lisa holding up some other unidentifiable object.

I broke down and cried.

We all decided not to tell my parents about the fire until they landed back in New York because they were really excited about going to California, and if they came home early, it wouldn't have changed anything. I went over to their place every day and cleaned, threw things away and tried to make it all as presentable as possible. Each day my guilt grew more and more, and I kept trying to think of how I could've prevented it. There was a fire extinguisher on the other side of Aunt Janet's door. If we got in there, maybe the damage could've been prevented or at least not as bad. The lie I told in the hospital with hopes of making things better … had caused this.

The day my parents and aunt returned, Eric and I picked them up from the airport. They were excited to tell us about their trip and did so the entire ride to Brooklyn. I was quiet, and Eric kept looking at me in between his "Oh, yeah" and "That sounds great" responses to Mom. When we pulled up to their house, Dad opened the car door and I said, "Wait, Dad, could you close the door for a second please?"

"Sure, what's up?" he said and closed the door.

Sigh.

I turned around in the passenger seat to face the three of them. "Um, there was an accident while you were away."

"What kind of accident?" asked Mom.

"There was a fire." I said.

"What?" "A fire?" "Where?"

"Umm ..." I said.

"There was a fire in the basement," Eric said. "It didn't get to the rest of the house, but—"

Dad jumped out of the car and ran into the house. My mother and aunt followed him. Eric and I joined them in the basement. My parents were flabbergasted. My Aunt Janet was on her knees and crying hysterically. I knelt down next to her and held her tight.

The next day, Mom and I went to Crate & Barrel to buy some items for Aunt Janet who was now staying in the guest room upstairs. The basement had been colorful and full of décor when Aunt Janet renovated it years ago, so we wanted to make the guest room the same for her. We also picked up basic items for her as well, since the only clothes and toiletries she now had were those she took to California.

When we got back to my parents, Aunt Janet was asleep on the sofa, so Mom and I went upstairs and revamped the guest room with all of the items we just purchased. When we were done, the room looked really great, like a mini version of Aunt Janet's former space. While Mom and I were cleaning up the bags and packaging, Aunt Janet appeared in the doorway.

"What do you think, Jan?" Mom asked.

Aunt Janet just nodded and walked away. Mom and I looked at each other, and she shrugged. I slumped in the chair.

"You're going to have to give her some time, Bailey. She lost a lot in the fire and just learned about it yesterday. She'll come around," said Mom. Then she patted my shoulder and left the room.

I just sat there and cried. *This is all my fault.*

A few minutes later, Aunt Janet came back into the room and saw me crying.

"Hey," she said, which was the most she'd spoken in the last twenty-four hours.

I quickly wiped my face.

"Why the tears?"

"I'm just … I'm just so sorry this happened." I tried to hold back the tears. The last thing I wanted was for her to feel sorry for *me.*

"It was my fault. Why are you crying?"

I just shook my head and wiped my eyes.

"Look," she said. "This room looks beautiful. You and your mom … you did a smashing job." She must've been drinking. She only spoke with a random accent when she'd had too many adult beverages.

"Aunt Jan—"

"No, no. No worries. I'll be just fine. Now go. Let me enjoy my new pad. Carry on." Then she pushed me out of the room and closed the door. I went downstairs and joined Mom in the kitchen.

"What?" asked Mom.

"Aunt Janet said she likes the room, but I think she's been drinking," I said.

Mom put her hand on her hip and sighed deeply. Then she began humming and washing dishes. She was mad.

"Mom?" No response. "Mom?"

"Yeah?"

"Are you okay?"

"It's getting late, Bailey. Why don't you go home and get some rest. You've got to work tomorrow," she said. Then she walked past me and left the kitchen. I went home.

For the next few weeks, I called Aunt Janet daily to see how her spirits were. I was too much of a coward to actually go by the house anymore, but I had to at least speak with her to see if she was feeling better. The conversations were usually short. Some days she sounded just fine and told me about her soap operas. Other days, I could tell that she'd been drinking and didn't know that it was me on the line.

I ordered tons of clothes and shoes for her online to replace what she'd lost until Mom told me there was no more room for the shipments, and I needed to stop. My aunt hired a crew who had begun work on repairing the basement, and

Mom said it was looking great, and you could no longer tell there'd been a fire there. This was good for my aunt and my dad, who was pissed about the incident and wasn't speaking to Aunt Janet. Mom was busy trying to find out how my aunt was getting alcohol into her room. Two months later, Dad found the liquor stashed in the guest bathroom down the hall—the one my parents never used. Once they solved that mystery, Aunt Janet remained sober for weeks and was able to deal with her loss the right way. Then she slowly became her old self again. I joined them for lunch one Saturday, and it was great.

"Olivia, look on your magic phone and tell me what the weather is in Milan," Aunt Janet said.

"Okay," said Olivia who giggled then performed the search on her phone.

"Why Milan, Jan?" Mom asked.

"I'm thinking of traveling and want to go somewhere fun. I got my new passport in the mail this week and have a travel bug now."

"It's the same as here, about forty degrees," said Olivia.

"Have you been to Italy at all, Aunt Janet?" I asked.

"Yes, but only to Rome. There was no fashion there," she said. *Oh, Aunt Janet …*

"Are you going to finish your sandwich, Olive?" I asked.

"No, you can have it," Olivia said, so I helped myself.

"Look who's got an appetite," said Aunt Janet. "You usually eat like a bird."

"Yeah, but this sandwich is good," I said.

"Good? It's bologna—all the bad parts of the animal. The butt, feet, penis—"

"Janet!" Mom said.

"You know it's true. Just because this brand cost a little more doesn't mean the pig was *neutered*."

"Oh gosh," said Mom.

Aunt Janet is back. Yay!

EXTRA! EXTRA!

My first month of pregnancy was a breeze, so I assumed that my first trimester would be a breeze as well. Nope. By my second month, I had morning sickness every day, and the fatigue kicked in by the end of my third month. Eric went to every doctor's appointment with me and, as promised, we were both home by six o'clock on weeknights. Leaving work on time was tough to do until the fatigue kicked in. Then 5:45 couldn't come soon enough.

I had only gained a few pounds by my thirteenth week, and my OB/GYN had expected me to weigh more. I told him that I was sleeping more than eating, but I was definitely eating. He said that it was still early, so he wasn't too concerned. *Plus the women in my family carried pretty small until about the seventh or eighth month — I didn't mention that though.* Other than that, everything was looking great, so we were free to share the news with our loved ones.

"Do you want to know the gender?" Dr. Green asked.

I replied no just as Eric replied yes.

"No, Eric. That changes everything. Let's just relish being pregnant for now."

"What about … baby shower colors and stuff?" he asked.

"Um hmm. Because you're concerned about baby shower colors," I replied as I stood up to leave. "Thank you, Dr. Green."

"You're welcome."

At the elevator Eric asked, "Bailey, do you really want to wait until delivery to find out if it's a boy or a girl?"

I decided to compromise, so he wouldn't feel like his contribution ended at implantation. "Okay, how about we find out the gender at the start of the third trimester since we're in the second trimester now?"

"Deal."

"That'll be just in time for baby shower colors, right?" I asked sarcastically.

"That's why it's a perfect plan."

Eric and I agreed to only tell family members and close friends. I told him that I didn't want anyone at work to know just yet, so not to mention it to anyone who may know a colleague.

I decided to tell my parents that weekend in person. But I couldn't wait to tell my Olivia, so I sent her a text message asking her to stop by after school, since I was working from home. She texted me back saying that she stopped by my office, but they told her that I wasn't in. I asked if everything was okay, and she said that she just wanted to see me.

When I got home from the doctor, I made a sandwich and got a lot of work accomplished. I knew that once Olivia arrived, I wouldn't get much else done after I told her the good news. Other than a little bump when I stood in front of my mirror naked, you still couldn't tell that I was pregnant.

I could so take a nap right now. What time is it? It's only three thirty, wow. Let me order Chinese food since Olivia will be here soon.

Twenty minutes later, Olivia and the food delivery were downstairs.

"How've you been?" I asked as we dug into the food.

"I'm good. I miss you. I haven't seen you in weeks."

"I know. I miss you too. Work has been so busy, but it's easing up."

"Good."

"Hey, do you know anyone who may know Gwen Stefani?"

"Um ... no. Why?"

"Never mind. Okay, Olivia I have a secret. And I know that you won't tell anyone at—"

"I won't tell anyone," she insisted. "What is it?"

"I'm having a baby."

"You are? Really?"

"I am."

"Oh my gosh!" she said and hugged me. "So how many months are you—is it a girl or boy? How do you feel?"

"I just started my second trimester. And I'm doing well. We don't know the sex of the baby yet."

"No?"

"No. I actually don't want to know, but your Uncle Eric wants to know."

"Is he here?" she whispered.

"No, he's not here. He knows I'm pregnant by the way," I joked.

"No, no. I was just wondering if he was here."

"No, just us." She got a little quiet after that.

"You okay?"

"Yes, I'm fine," she replied and then perked up. "So, do you want a boy or a girl?"

"I want a healthy baby, of course."

"Of course."

"But I do want a healthy *baby girl*."

"Me too! I hope it's a girl. I'll babysit all the time and take her everywhere. You sure you don't want to find out what you're having?"

"I will, just not now. In a couple of months."

"Okay, cool."

"You said that you stopped by my office today. Is everything okay?"

"No, that was nothing. It was my lunch break, and I wanted to see you, that's all."

I only partially believed her, but I wouldn't push for now. We ate and talked for a couple more hours. "Your Uncle Eric will be home soon, and he can give you a ride home."

"No, that's okay," Olivia replied and hopped up. "I can take the train. I have my MetroCard."

"No. Why take the train? He can take you."

"That's okay, Aunt B," she insisted and grabbed her book bag. "Really, I can take the train."

"Okay, okay. Ms. Independent." I walked with her to the door. "I'm telling the family about the baby this weekend. So you won't have to keep the secret too long."

"Okay. I won't say a word, though."
"That's my girl."

Eric got home a bit late, and we talked about our day while we cuddled on the couch.

"Do you want some Chinese food? There are leftovers in the fridge."

"I'm fine for now, thanks. My assistant gave her notice today."

"Gretchen? Oh no. Why?"

"Her husband retired last year, and she wants to take it easy and be home with him."

"Well, I can understand that."

"Yeah. But she keeps me organized and manages all of my endless paperwork. It'll be hard to replace her."

"You could get a temp for a little while."

"I'm cautious about having just anybody come into the office. There's a lot of confidential information all over the place. A referral would be good. I'll put some feelers out there."

"That's a good idea. I'll let you know if I come across anyone too." Elly actually assisted Eric at his office some time ago when she was between jobs and before Gretchen was hired. *I think someone else about Gretchen's age would be a suitable replacement.*

"Thanks. I'll have to go out of town for a few days next week. I'm hoping she can stay around until then."

"Out of town? For how long?"

"Just two or three days to DC; I'll try and make it two days," he said and caressed my face.

"Okay, two days isn't too bad, I guess. Olivia stopped by, and I told her about the baby."

"Oh yeah? I know she must be excited."

"Very. I couldn't wait to tell her," I said. "You look tired. Are you okay?"

"Yeah, yeah I'm fine. You know what though, I'm going to take a hot shower." He gave me a peck on the forehead. "And then maybe I'll have some of that Chinese food."

"Okay." I fell asleep on the sofa until the next morning.

REVELATIONS

It was the weekend, and I'd been getting ready to go to my parent's house. I looked for a shirt that showed my belly bump *at least a little*, but I wasn't having any luck.

Eric stood in the closet doorway and shook his head. "You know, most women *want* to look small when they're pregnant," he said.

"I know. I don't want to look big just …" I threw another shirt on the floor, "a little pregnant."

"Well, pregnant lady, we need to leave in fifteen minutes if I'm going to make it to Brooklyn and then back to Jersey in time."

"Okay, I'll just wear this one. I'm almost ready. Give me ten minutes."

"Okie dokie."

Eric dropped me off at my parents. Lisa's car was parked out front. *Oh brother!*

I walked in and there were several boxes in the living room.

"Hello?" I called out.

"Hey," Mom said, surprised to see me.

"What are all of these boxes?"

Lisa joined us and said, "This is all of Aunt Janet's stuff."

"Aunt Janet's stuff? Why is her stuff in boxes?"

Mom sighed and sat on the sofa.

I had a bad feeling. I sat next to her.

"Honey, your Aunt Janet is moving out."

"What? Why, because of what happened?"

"No. She's just getting her own place on Long Island, that's all." Then Mom left the room.

Lisa shrugged.

"Something had to have happened." "I guess she's not saying," Lisa said. Then Mom walked back into the room.

"Mom, come on. What happened?" I asked.

"Nothing happened. She wasn't going to live here forever." *Lies. Of course she was.* They were both going to outlive Dad and paint the entire house pink. Everybody knew that. Mom didn't fess up, and she was obviously upset about it.

"Where's Aunt Janet now?"

"She's out."

"Where's Dad?"

"He's volunteering at the vet center."

"Have you seen her new place? How is it? Is she going to live alone?"

"Not now, Bailey," Mom said and left the room again.

I stared at the ceiling. It was quiet.

"I have to pee," I said. When I went back into the living room, Mom was there.

"How are you feeling, Mom?" I asked.

"I'm fine. I'm good."

"At the end of the day, you have to be happy, Mom," said Lisa. *She knew something.*

"Why wouldn't Mom be happy if Aunt Janet stayed here?"

"She's not saying that I wouldn't be happy," Mom chimed in.

"Well, no one is saying anything! What's going on?" No one said a word.

"Okay, then," I said and stood up. "I'm going to head out."

"Wait, where are you going?" asked Mom.

"I'm heading home," I said and headed toward the door.

Mom followed and asked, "Why? You just got here; why are you leaving?"

"I just want to go home now and lie down. You said you're okay, right? And nothing is going on, right? So, I'll see you later."

"Bailey," she said as I opened the door. I walked out onto the front stoop. "Wait, did you come by for something?"

I whispered, "Just to tell you that I'm pregnant."

"What! Oh my God," she said and squeezed me tight. "You're pregnant? My goodness!" I didn't want my sister to hear — *too late for that now.* "Come on, come back inside. Tell me everything," Mom insisted.

"Not today, Mom. I'm not up for it anymore."

"Please, honey. Stay," she said and stared at me, hoping I'd give in. "Go lie down upstairs and take a nap. You look tired."

"Thanks."

"No, you look great, just a little fatigued. Come take a nap." Then she whispered, "When you wake up, your sister will be gone, and we can chat. Okay?"

I paused and then said, "Okay." When I got back inside, I didn't see Lisa. I went upstairs and fell asleep almost as soon as my face hit the pillow.

A few hours later, I woke up to the delicious smell of baked apple pie. *Yum!* I sat up in bed and remembered the last time I was in there and the many, many tears that I shed. *Let me get out of this room.*

I headed downstairs hoping that Lisa had indeed left and walked into the living room. The boxes were gone. I wondered where they were and what part of the story their absence represented. I went downstairs to the basement and looked around. It was better than new, but it was empty. I went back upstairs.

"Mom?" I called out.

"Back here, honey." She was out back on the deck.

"It's drizzling out here, Mom," I said standing in the doorway.

"I know. I just love to sit out here sometimes though," she said then came back inside. I put my arm around her shoulder, and she put her arm around my waist. We went to the kitchen, and she brought two plates to the table.

"Do you have ice cream?"

"Sure do." She pulled out some vanilla ice cream.

"Perfect." She cut pieces of pie for us and my piece was way too big. "Mom!"

"Eat what you want and save the rest," she said as she *always* said when she was overfeeding you.

I *a la mode*d both of our slices, and we dug in.

"So you and Eric are going to be parents?" Mom said happily.

"Yes, we are," I sang. "I'm thirteen weeks."

"Wow! You look great, honey. Eric must be thrilled. How do you feel?"

"He is and I'm fine. The morning sickness didn't last long, but I'm glad it's over. I'm just always tired. But my doctor said that everything looks good."

"Good. And what about being pregnant with the … amnesia?"

First time she'd said that word in a while.

"My neurologist has been working with my OB/GYN, and there have been no reasons to be concerned."

"Perfect. You don't look pregnant at all."

"I know. I look in the mirror every day to see if the bump is more visible. My doctor says that I'm kinda small, but he's not worried, he was just saying." Not sure if I was trying to convince Mom or myself.

"Let me see." I stood up and raised my shirt. "Yeah, I see it," she said and rubbed my stomach.

"I don't know what the gender is yet. I know you're going to ask."

"That *was* my next question. Do you want to know?"

"I don't but Eric does. I want to be surprised. I want to be surprised with a girl."

"I bet Eric wants a boy."

"Yep."

"Daughters are great."

"Aren't they!"

"They are. Especially when they're getting along." *She had me there.*

"Yeah," was all that I could come up with. That was another conversation for another day. I should ask her if she and Aunt Janet were getting along, but I wouldn't dare do that. I wanted so badly to know what happened, though. We chatted more about the pregnancy; she told me about her experiences and gave me advice.

I worried about her living in this big house without my Aunt Janet. They were best friends, and Dad had tons of his own activities. I didn't want her to get lonely. I wanted to ask specifics about what happened, but I didn't want that topic to be on her mind when I left, and I knew that Eric would be there to get me soon. I needed to leave her with happy thoughts.

"Will you help me think of some girl names, Mom?"

"Sure, but shouldn't you wait until you know it's a girl for sure?"

"We could do boys names too."

"You wouldn't just name him Eric, Jr.?" *No, but I'm sure you would, Mom.*

I dodged her question. "Oh—I need to search for a nanny since I don't know how long it'll take to secure a good one."

"Hmm … You know, I would love to take care of the baby. Even if it's just part-time, so you'll only need a part-time nanny."

"Really, Mom?" I asked excitedly. It would be great bonding for us.

"Of course. It would be my joy. I could take the train into the city. You know I love the train, and all I have is time nowadays since I'm retired."

"Mom, I would love that more than anything. I know Eric would too."

"Oh good. Oh this is going to be so nice."

I didn't know who was more excited, Mom or me—okay, I was. This was such a great idea. I'd trust her more than anyone with my baby, and I'd get to see her regularly, so I wouldn't worry as much about her being in this house without Aunt Janet. And we'd become best buds again. *Perfect.*

"Is Dad back yet?"

"He was, but then he went to get a haircut." That gave me an idea.

"Do you have milk?" *They never have milk.*

"No, I don't. Do you want some?"

"Yeah, warm milk would go great with this pie."

"Better than ice cream?"

"Not better. I'm just craving some warm milk. I'll walk over to the corner store and get some."

"I'll come with you."

"No, that's okay. I'll just run there quickly and come right back. You might stop and talk to everyone."

"Okay, hurry back."

I walked down the street and into the barbershop. Dad was sitting in a chair against the wall with a couple of other guys. He either had his hair cut an hour ago or would get it cut in about an hour. Those guys could sit and talk there forever. Dad was a gentle giant, standing at six feet tall, with a short grey beard. Mom said that having daughters softened him up a bit from the hard exterior he'd formed in the army. Now he was just a kind, hug-giving, retired engineer with a basketball addiction.

"Well, look who we have here," said Tony, the owner of the barbershop.

"Hi." *I have to keep it simple. I shouldn't remember any of these people.*

"Hey, Bailey. What's going on?" my dad said. All the male conversation ceased.

"Hi, Dad." I took his arm and walked him toward the back of the shop. Once we reached the back, the men resumed talking.

"Is everything okay?" he asked.

"I guess. Mom told me about Aunt Janet and why she moved out." This wasn't *totally* untrue. My mom was going to tell me ... someday. I was *fore*telling.

"She did?" I nodded. "I didn't think she'd do that. It's all just a mess."

Since I really didn't know what happened, I didn't know how to respond so I just said, "Did she have to move out just because of that, though?"

"Your mother was mad. I've never seen her that angry before. I think she was more upset that your aunt didn't tell her about the fifteen-minute delay in calling 911 after the accident, you know."

I'm confused, but I just nodded.

"Your mother forgave her for being the driver once you came out of the coma and everything," he continued, "but she couldn't explain why she didn't call 911 immediately. That delay could have killed you, and it's the reason you fell into the coma in the first place. It was just a big mess."

Oh my God! Aunt Janet was driving me the night of the accident? And then she didn't immediately call 911? What the hell! That's why Mom didn't want to talk to me about it. Had Aunt Janet been drunk?

It was Christmas, but I didn't remember anything from that night. "How did all of this even come up, Dad?"

"Your aunt had a little too much to drink yesterday, and your mother started talking to her again about slowing down and getting some help. Next thing your aunt got offended and lashed out. Then she apologized, which led to her crying uncontrollably and confessing to your mother. That's when she told her. Your mother almost ripped her face off. I had to get between the two of them. Then your mother told her to be out by the morning, and she was. I had your brother bring some boxes over, and we packed your aunt up."

"When I saw the boxes at first, I thought it had something to do with the fire."

"No. But that incident didn't help, of course."

"Right. And now she's on Long Island."

"Long Island? Who said that?"

"Mom."

"I don't think your mother knows where she is. I think she went to stay with one of your sisters, but I may be wrong. Your brother drove her stuff over to her. I didn't ask a thing."

"Hmm ..." I just stared ahead trying to process everything. *I need to call Aunt Janet first thing in the morning. She must feel terrible.*

Then Dad nudged me. "You okay?" he asked.

"Yeah, I better head back to the house."

"Come on. I'll head back with you."

"Dad?"

"Yeah?"

"Do you know anyone who may know Gwen Stefani?" *Job-preservation mode — no stone unturned.*

"Yeah."

"You do?" *I was in total shock.*

"Yeah. Rob's son, the drummer, he knows Stefani," he said. Then my dad turned to a guy in the barber's seat and said, "Robert, your boy knows Stefani, right?"

"Yeah, why?" said Rob.

"My daughter's asking." Then my dad turned to me.

"You need carpet laid, hon?" asked Rob.

"Carpet laid? No. I need to get in touch with *Gwen Stefani,* the singer."

"Singer?" Rob said.

"Singer?" my dad said. "I thought you meant Gwenaldo Stefani, the floor guy."

"No, not ... Come on, Dad." I took his arm, waved to Rob and we left.

"Dad?"

"Yeah?"

"I'm having a baby."

"Is that a Stefani song or —"

"No," I chuckled. "I'm pregnant, Dad." *He stopped in his tracks.*

"What? Honey, that's great news! Wow," he said and hugged me. "Did you tell your mother?"

"Yeah, I did."

"She must be over the moon."

"She is."

"Wow, another grandbaby. We can never have too many of those." He tried to hold my hand as we crossed the street. He's done it out of habit since I was a little girl. This time I let him. "A baby!"

THIS JUST IN

My sixth month of pregnancy was a breeze, and I finally had a discernible bump. I told Christina I was pregnant, and she was ecstatic. Since she had two little ones she absolutely adored—I adored them too, actually—she was delighted that I was *joining the club*. I asked her not to tell anyone, since I was still hoping to get the senior manager role after the LA project. Who would be promoted at the project's completion—Stephen or me—was still to be determined. And I hadn't produced Gwen yet to Dennis, who actually stopped asking me about it, so I still had a lot of impressing to do with my actual skills.

The beginning of my third trimester had been difficult. I overdid it with travel to California, but I got to see my brother Stewart and his family a few times so it was worth it. And Eric and I both began to break the "be home by six o'clock" rule by month five. I worked late about four nights a week but that was after Eric started having all of these work trips so there was no reason for me to rush home. And, if he was home, he was in the den.

"How's Dallas?" I asked Eric, who'd just called me.

"It's okay. The trip has been productive but I wish I was there with you, cuddling, or rubbing your feet." *When's the last time that happened when you were home?*

"Yeah, me too. I miss you."

"I'll be home tomorrow and in time for your check-up the day after."

"You haven't missed one yet."

"I promised you that I wouldn't."

The day of my check-up, I woke up with severe back pains. I wanted to stay in bed so badly, but we were supposed to find out the gender of the baby, and I had two huge meetings that I couldn't afford to miss. I still wanted the gender of the baby to be a delivery-day revelation, *but* if we were having a girl, that delicious tidbit would get me through this pain today.

Eric and I entered Dr. Green's office, and after my examination, he said I had excess fluid. I asked if the baby looked okay, and he said that the baby was great. Then he asked me if I'd been having any pain, and I told him I was fine. Eric looked at me quickly, remembering the pain that I woke up with that morning and the previous week. So the doctor asked Eric, "How's she doing?"

"Well," Eric said, "She's been having back pain and trouble sleeping." *Snitch.*

"I'm going to need you to head home as soon as you leave here, and I need you in bed for the next five days," he said.

"Five days?"

"Yes, five days. You're not twenty-two anymore, and I'm going to need you to take care of yourself and this baby."

"Okay." *Ugh.*

"And I'll need to see you on day six to check on that fluid and see if the back pain persists."

"Okay, six days."

"So ..." Eric said, "it's gender-learning-time."

"That it is," Dr. Green said. "Are you both ready to find out?"

"Absolutely," Eric said.

"Sure," I said.

The doctor showed us a printout of the sonogram and said, "It's a bit fuzzy and the baby's positioning makes it a bit difficult to see but it looks like you two are having ... a boy."

"Yes!" Eric said.

"Wow," I said. *Aww, no little dresses.* "Well, he looks healthy, right?"

"Yes, everything looks great. I could try again in a few minutes and see if the baby repositions—"

"No, that's okay," I said. I needed to go.

We made our way to the elevator while several young nurses snuck a peek at Eric.

"I know you wanted a girl, sweetie."

"Oh, it's okay. The baby is healthy. What more can we ask for, right?"

"Right. But you'll see, when he gets here and stares into your eyes, you're gonna melt. Mark my words."

"I know. It'll be great."

When we got downstairs, Eric hailed me a taxi and said, "See you tonight. I may be late but be sure to get some rest."

"You're going to be late tonight?"

"Yeah, without Gretchen everything has been totally disorganized. Documents are missing, I don't know where anything is; it's crazy. Sorry sweetie!" he said running to another taxi. *Ugh.*

I was supposed to go home but wanted to pop into work quickly first. The meetings that week were the final ones, which would determine who got promoted. I couldn't miss this one ... and, actually, I shouldn't miss tomorrow's meeting either. I'd been doing a great job, but I really needed to impress in these meetings. I finally told Dennis that Gwen Stefani had *conflicting interests and couldn't be our spokesperson* once I heard back from my last Facebook contact and didn't get a callback from Gwen's cousins or yoga instructor's sister. Dennis was actually okay and said he had something else up his sleeve just in case. I was relieved.

Two and a half hours later, the meeting ended, and I headed straight to the bathroom to pee. Then I went to check-in with Carrie before heading home and she said that Olivia was sitting in my office waiting for me. When I saw Olivia's face, I knew that my day was about to change. I closed the door behind me.

"Hi baby. What's wrong?" I sat next to her.

"I didn't want to say anything last time because you were so happy about being pregnant," she said emotionally.

"What last time? Say anything about what, Olivia?"

Her eyes began to swell. "I saw Uncle Eric in New Jersey with Miss Elly." And then the tears fell. She and I just looked at each other.

A CHANCE TO LIE

I don't even need to ask specifics because I know what she's inferring.

She continued, "My class was at the New Jersey Performing Arts Center, and they were there too seeing another show. They were holding hands and … kissing." She could hardly get her words out now, so I held her and just let her cry in my arms. I knew that it must've been so hard for her to tell me this. All I wanted in that moment was to restore her innocence. She'd been unfairly exposed to scandal, and I saw the guilt of that knowledge in her eyes. It killed me.

Why did I think he would change? I'm so stupid.

Olivia sat up and wiped her eyes.

"What did you mean by last time, sweetie? You saw your uncle and her before?"

She nodded.

"I know it wasn't easy to tell me this, Olivia," I said as I held her face. "But thank you for telling me. You know that I love you, right?"

She nodded and started to cry again. I held her, and we sat there for a few minutes. Then Christina opened my door and was about to say something, but stopped in her tracks when she saw us.

"I'm sorry," Christina said and backed out. "I'll come back." I nodded and then she left.

"I'm sorry, Aunt B."

"You have nothing to be sorry for. I'll be okay," I said and wiped her face. "You have to head back to school."

"I know," she said reluctantly, and didn't move. I moved her hair out of her face and gave her an "it's time to go" look.

She stood up slowly as I rubbed her back. I grabbed my purse and handed her a twenty-dollar bill.

"I know that you probably missed lunch already."

"I don't need twenty dollars."

I waved my hand and said, "Keep it."

"Thank you."

"Guess what?"

She turned around and said, "What?"

"I'm having a boy."

"Yeah? Baby boys are cute too."

"Yeah, they are."

She waved and left. I sat at my desk chair and felt rage coming to the surface. My back was starting to hurt again.

Christina poked her head in my office and asked, "Is everything okay?"

"Not really. But I can't think about or talk about it right now." I rubbed my stomach.

"Are you feeling okay?"

"I'll be fine. I'm heading home, though. But call me if you need me. Don't tell anyone I'm gone unless they ask."

"Of course. Let me know if you need anything, okay?"

"I will. Thanks, Christina."

While I was in the taxi, Mom sent me a text message and asked about a baby shower. I asked if she'd plan it and also told her that I was having a boy. She was happy and agreed to take care of all the shower planning. *Good, I have other things to plan.*

When I got home, I saw a suitcase in the foyer. I forgot that Eric was traveling again tonight. *Perfect. That'll prevent me from killing him in his sleep, for the next couple of days anyway.* I kicked off my shoes and headed straight for the bedroom. I fell asleep immediately.

A few hours later, maybe a few more than that, the big bright moon outside awakened me. I got up and saw that Eric's suitcase was gone. *Good.* I skimmed through my email to see if there were any updates about the LA project. Nothing. Everything else could wait until tomorrow.

My back felt much better too. *Rest, hmm.* My doctor was right.

I checked the refrigerator, but there was nothing that I felt like eating. I skimmed through my missed calls and text messages. I had a text from my friend Bryce who wanted to see if Christina and I were going to go to his firm's party next week, so I decided to give him a call.

"I hope you're not calling to tell me that you're not coming to my party."

"No, no. Christina and I will be there for sure."

"Okay, good. So what've you been up to? I haven't seen you since Tyler's birthday dinner." Tyler was Christina's husband.

"I know, right. It's been a minute. Hey, have you eaten yet? Do you want to grab dinner?"

"I've been waiting for this day, you know. Should we go somewhere romantic?" he joked.

"Ha ha. I'm pregnant, remember?"

"Yeah—not a deal breaker. How far along are you again?"

"Mr. Funny Man."

"No, you know me; I'm still in the office and haven't eaten yet. Let's grab a bite."

"Great. Would you mind coming to my side of town? I'm trying to limit my mobility."

"No problem. How about that Italian spot?"

"Perfect. What time?"

"Meet you there in twenty minutes."

Bryce got to the restaurant as soon as I did, and we walked in together after sharing a hug.

"You look great."

"Thanks, so do you," I said after brushing his lapel with my hand.

We were seated and gave our orders.

I sipped my water as Bryce asked, "So how's the fake amnesia life been treating you? I'm sorry, I mean *faux-nesia*."

"Har har."

"What's wrong?"

I sighed and said, "Everything here forward is confidential."

"Of course."

"Super, Christina-doesn't-even-know-it-yet confidential," I added.

"Okay."

"I'm divorcing Eric, and I'd like for you to draw up the paperwork for me," I blurted out. "But before that even, I need for you to check into his assets in case he's hiding anything."

He didn't blink. Then he said, "I'm so sorry."

"Yeah …"

"What happened?"

"Cheated. Cheating. And with someone who was very close to me."

He sighed. "All this *and* pregnant? How are you holding up?"

I shrug. "I'm dealing ... I'm angry. I was stupid to think he'd change just because I got pregnant."

"Not stupid. Hopeful. You wanted to hold on to your marriage."

"I guess ... Anyway, I want out, and I want you to help me."

"Then consider it done. I can find out as much as you'd like or just enough to—"

"Find out everything, every single dirty thing that you can."

"Okay, then." He raised his glass. "To getting you everything you deserve and more."

I raised my glass to his. "Cheers."

Bryce started as a corporate attorney, then he went into family law and was now an entertainment attorney, but he had attorneys of all types at his practice. He was divorced— no, not divorced; he was engaged a few years back then his fiancé called it off, due to his being married to his job. *And she wasn't into polygamy.* He was laid back for an attorney and was about five feet eleven, slim built with a teeny gut and, even though he was balding, his confidence and personality drew you in. Like me, he also came from a big family—he had four sisters.

"Remember that intern who used to say 'cheers' after everything?" he asked.

"Yes. That and use air quotes at the wrong time."

"That's right. I forget what country he was from, but he didn't understand anything. Ever." *That was so true.* "Man, I miss working with you guys."

"Yeah, we used to have a ball. Do you still drink eight cups of coffee a day?"

"Yep—five by noon."

I shook my head, looked closer at him, and said, "Wait, you're wearing glasses! I didn't even notice."

"Yeah, too many nights reading tiny print in low light."

"So, not old age?" I joked. He gave me a *smrown*. "Oooh, and they're Prada. Look at you," I said.

"They are nice, huh? Don't they make me look smart?"

"They're designer glasses not magic glasses, Bryce."

"Yeah ... Not missing working with you so much anymore." The waitress appeared with our *Insalata Caprese* appetizer.

The next morning, I woke up in pain again and took my time getting up. When I finally got showered and dressed, it was almost nine o'clock. My cell phone rang. *Christina.*

"Hi there. I'm on my way, had a late start."

"Hey," she said as if she'd had a tough morning.

"What's wrong?"

She paused and said, "Apparently there was another private meeting last night."

"Okay."

"They chose Stephen for the senior manager position." I felt the pain creeping back into my back. I didn't have any words. Then Christina said, "Bailey?"

"Yeah, I'm here. Um … I'm going to work from home today, actually," I replied. She was quiet on the other end. I'm sure she felt bad about the situation.

"Call me, okay? Call me if you need anything at all. Do you want me to bring you some lunch later?"

"No, I'll be fine. Thanks, Christina."

I sat on my bed and cried. Everything I'd been working on for the last few months was crumbling before me. I got under the covers, closed my eyes, and slept.

I woke up at about three o'clock, reached over to the radio and let it play loud. I changed into comfy pajamas and then got a large glass of orange juice. *What I would give for wine right now.* I leaned against the kitchen island, sipped my juice, and thought about my life. I felt like crawling under a rock, but I knew I had to be strategic. I had less than two months before the baby arrived. I knew for sure I didn't want to be under the same roof with Eric by then. Bryce would be working on the divorce paperwork and looking into Eric's assets, so that was in motion. I'd check in with Bryce in a few days, if I didn't hear from him first. I felt like a silly old-school wife to not already know about our assets. Eric had kept me in the dark, and I let him.

I needed to figure out what to do about work. I didn't get the senior manager position. *I really, really wanted it.* Being at work was going to be difficult. I called my doctor and told him that I woke up with more back pain, and he put me on bed rest for a month. I asked him to send me documentation that I could forward to the HR department at knirD, so that I could officially be on medical leave while I got over my defeat and planned my next steps. I was sure Dennis would think, *"I knew she couldn't handle it,"* but I didn't care anymore.

I sent an email to Carrie and then texted Christina that I'd be out. She was glad because she knew I'd been working in pain. She insisted on bringing me dinner knowing that Eric was out of town. I happily agreed. My cell phone rang. *Olivia.*

"I've been thinking about you all day."

"You're so sweet. I really am fine. I stayed home from work today and got some rest, and Christina is going to bring me dinner later."

"Okay, good," she said. "When I got home yesterday, I went into super baby shower research and planning. I'm helping Grandma."

"Good, so everything won't have flowers on it," I joked.

"No, I won't let that happen. Quick question, what about your registry?"

"Ugh. I don't want to do it. Can you do it for me? Or ask grandma please?"

"Actually, my mom offered to help with the registry if that's okay."

What? My sister wants to help with my baby shower? "That would be great, Olivia. Tell her that I said thank you."

"Okay, I will. Okay, that's it. I'm going to come and check on you this weekend, okay?"

"That would be wonderful."

Now all I could think about was my sister offering to help with the registry of my baby shower. That little piece of information brightened up my day. I hoped it was the beginning of … something.

THE SHOWER

So, a couple of weeks had passed, and now it was the day of my baby shower. I dreamt that I invited Eric to the shower and served him with the divorce papers in front of everyone. My brothers beat him up, and my mother actually sided with me. It was quite dramatic. Luckily, Bryce had been working on something and asked me to hold off saying anything to Eric yet, so even if I was tempted to, I couldn't. It was agonizing being under the same roof with him knowing about him and Elly. I asked him to sleep in the guest room blaming it on pregnancy discomfort. That helped some because I just stayed in my room all day. And when Olivia visited me, she didn't want to be around him anyway, so it was perfect.

All I seemed to do was sleep most days. It helped a lot with alleviating my back pain, but I wondered if I was depressed. I wished I could have spoken with Christina, but I had to keep the divorce quiet while Bryce conducted his investigation. I really hadn't felt like celebrating today. I just wanted to stay in bed. Then Olivia called.

"Everything is set up, and most of the people are here. I'm going to come upstairs and get you okay?" Olivia asked. We were having the baby shower in my building's clubroom, a beautiful space that residents can rent for events.

"All right."

"Are you okay?"

"Yeah." *She can tell I'm not.* "Come up whenever you're ready, sweetie."

I stood in front of the mirror to make sure I was presentable. I looked nice. New pretty dress, the only weight gain was in my stomach; I had my hair and makeup done, and I wore the new bracelet that I ordered online. But I felt like crying. I sat back on the bed.

"Aunt B?" Olivia called as she keyed into my apartment.

"I'm in here," I said and wiped my eyes.

"You look so pretty! Oh my gosh!" she said.

"Thank you. Honestly, I just feel like staying in bed, Olivia."

She moved a piece of hair out of my face and said, "I know" very softly. She was only seventeen, but she seemed to know just how I was feeling. "Everyone is actually here, and they can't wait to see you. Your registry is completely empty. Every item has been purchased. And some of your favorite foods await you downstairs."

That sounded nice, actually. *No wine for me, but I'll deal.*

"Okay, then. Let's go."

Olivia took my arm and walked me to the clubroom. I could hear the guest's voices and light music. I could smell the delicious food too. Then I realized I hadn't eaten anything all day, and the baby must have smelled the food too because he started moving. I got to the doorway, and everyone cheered for me. It was so sweet and overwhelming at the same time. I started to tear up like a little punk. I guess I hadn't thought about actually *enjoying* the shower, so all the cheerful faces and encouragement had caught me off-guard.

I looked around the room, and I saw all of my family members, including my sister Lisa, some of my college friends, and friends from other circles. I had asked Olivia not to invite anyone from work because they had had a baby shower for me there already last month, with the exception of Christina who came, of course. Then I noticed everyone was wearing white. *What a nice touch!* It looked beautiful — everything looked beautiful. Olivia and my mom had really outdone themselves. Then my Aunt Janet walked into the room. *Wow!* I hadn't seen her since before she moved out of my parents' place. I'd spoken to her a few times, but it would be good to sit with her and chat today. She sat at the opposite end of the room from Mom. *Smart move.*

I sat in my assigned chair, which was adorned with beautiful white flowers, and I couldn't take my eyes off this little baby girl my friend Tracy held in her lap — the most adorable little baby I'd ever seen. *And she was looking at me too.*

"May I?" I asked Tracy.

"She doesn't go to anyone she doesn't know without crying," Tracy warned me before attempting to hand me her baby. I sat her in my lap. She looked at her mom, looked at me, looked back at her mom, and then laid her head on my chest while she sucked her finger. *Victory!* I had no intention of ever giving this baby back. I wondered if I snuck out of there with her if anyone would notice. *I shouldn't have worn heels. Wait, isn't Tracy's husband a judge? Ah, well. I'd have to enjoy this little baby for today alone.*

"So what are you having?" asked someone from the back of the room. And she stood so everyone could hear her.

"I don't know yet," I replied. I looked over at Olivia, and she winked at me. *Teaching my niece to lie, awesome. Tomorrow it's parallel parking and identity theft.*

"When are you due?" the woman continued.

"I have about a month to go," I replied. Then I got *oohs* and *ahhs* from the room.

"What? No way. You look great!" she said.

"Aw, thank you," I replied. "My doctor thinks I may deliver sooner, though."

"Does your doctor have you on bed rest?" Tracy asked.

"Yes. I hated it at first but it got rid of my back pain and forced me to take it easy."

"What do you hope you're having?" the woman persisted.

I waved Olivia over and whispered in her ear, "Let's end this round of Jeopardy and open gifts please."

"But that's not next on the agenda," Olivia replied.

I tilted my head.

"Gifts it is," she said and hurried to the front of the room and announced to everyone that we'd now be opening gifts. She asked the wait staff to serve the hors d'oeuvres as well. *Fancy shmancy.*

I got some amazing gifts. I looked at Lisa halfway through the gift-opening portion and mouthed "thank you" to her. She nodded. *Today is turning out to be really nice.* I had Olivia do the gift opening for me because I refused to hand

Tracy back her baby. And Tracy didn't seem to mind the freedom. She enjoyed herself and bounced around to nearly everyone in the room, not checking on her daughter once. With my free hand, I took tons of photos with my phone, though there was a photographer there.

After the gift opening, we watched a short video montage that Olivia and my mom had put together of photos and video clips of me from when I was younger until now. It was nothing normal—a concoction of some hilariously embarrassing moments throughout the years—braces with headgear, while singing and dancing; my kindergarten *talent* show, I use the word "talent" very loosely; my prom night in a hot pink stretch velvet dress; clips of my siblings tricking and scaring me, I was always an easy target; and when I said the wrong name at the altar on my wedding day—*that should've been my sign*. The guests really enjoyed it. And I loved it. Mom explained each scene to the guests in the room. It was really for me, though, because of my *amnesia*, which she never brought up in public ... or private actually.

Right after that, a police officer entered the room, and everyone got quiet. He immediately ripped off his clothes with one grab of the hand and then proceeded to gyrate the hell out of the guest closest to the door while in his undies, leaving us all speechless. There wasn't any music playing; it was just a room full of women with their mouths open and a couple of children. Olivia was next to me, so I managed to pull her to me and cover her eyes. And then seconds later, a woman ran into the room and grabbed the man, saying, "No, not this room! One floor up!" She pulled him out and then came back in, grabbed his clothes off the floor and ran back out again. The room filled with laughter. My mother couldn't contain herself; she was all red in the face and needed a glass of water. And then Jessica, a college friend, touched up her lipstick and said, "I'll be right back."

Yeah, she's not coming back. She'll be one floor up 'til the real cops come knocking.

And then, the loud woman said, "This is the best baby shower!"

By the end of the night, everyone was in good spirits. All the guests went home with a beautiful parting gift bag; my brother Chuck brought all of the gifts upstairs for me before driving Mom home.

"Can I stay the night with you, Aunt B?" Olivia asked as the final guests were leaving.

"Absolutely," I said. "I couldn't have asked for a more perfect baby shower, Olivia. Thank you *sooo* much."

"Anything for you."

I looked for my sister a couple of times when I saw that guests were starting to leave, but I didn't see her. Then, once the final guest left, I realized my sister was already gone. *Not even a good-bye. Wow. That won't ruin my mood, though. Today ended up being awesome.*

As Olivia and I walked toward the elevator, I asked, "Who was the loud woman with all the questions?"

"That was my mom's friend from work. She wanted there to be someone here that she knew."

"Other than her sister, daughter, mom, and aunt?"

Olivia shrugged.

"Anyway ..." I said. "Everyone wearing white, the food, the cake, the decorations, the video—oh, I loved it! You really made my day and made me excited to be a mom, Olivia."

"Really?"

"Really. It couldn't have been better."

"I'm so glad you liked it and everything turned out as planned." We opened the door and saw the living room filled with gifts.

"Oh, boy," I said looking at the stacks.

"Wow," Olivia added. "It didn't look like that much downstairs."

"I know."

"Well, at least the baby's room is painted. One less thing."

"True. I'm exhausted. Are you hungry? You must be exhausted too."

"I'm okay. Do you want anything?"

"I'm fine. Just need to shower, my bed, and I'll see you in the morning."

The next morning I woke up with the sun and, of course, a strong desire to pee. I wondered why Olivia hadn't slept in my bed so I went to look for her and saw a light on in the baby's room. When I peeked in, I saw wall ornaments up, stuffed animals, baby clothes hanging and folded in the drawers, little carpet and toy chest out, lamps, rocking chair—everything was done. It was beautiful, and I was speechless. Olivia must have been up all night working on it.

This little girl is something else.

I walked into the living room, and there was gift-wrap, gift bags, boxes, and tissue paper all over the place. And behind it all was little Olivia knocked out on the sofa. I wanted to wake her up and squeeze her but she had to be drained after the baby shower and now the baby's room. So, I just covered her with a blanket.

She is without a doubt my most favorite person in the entire world.

DEEPER THAN LUST

A few days later, I got a call from Bryce whom I'd anxiously anticipated hearing from.

"I hope you're calling with good news. Are the papers drawn?"

"I need to talk to you," he said seriously.

"Sure, what's up?"

"Can you come to my office?"

"Now?" I asked, looking down at my stained pajamas and slippers.

"Yeah, now. Sorry."

"Um, sure. I can be there in twenty minutes."

"Good, see you then," he said and hung up.

I looked at the phone and rushed to my bedroom—by rushed I mean waddled quickly—and changed from my pajamas to a pair of leggings and a sweatshirt. I pulled my hair back in a ponytail, put on my Tory Burch flats, my denim jacket, and left. Then I was stuck in traffic, only a block away from home and not moving at all.

Forty-five minutes later, I was at Bryce's office, and he met me at the elevator.

"What's up?" I asked. The suspense was killing me.

"Follow me," he said. And then he was off to his office. By off, I mean sprinted, off, gone.

"Slow down!" I said after he'd turned one too many corners for a pregnant woman, and I had no idea where he went.

"Sorry," he said, and peeked around the corner. He took my arm and walked at my pace until we got to his office. There were tons of papers, folders, and photos on his desk.

"Well? You're killing me here. Tell me something," I said.

"Where do I start? Okay. As we already knew, Eric and Elly have been … anyway, we learned the reason behind it."

"We?"

"Yeah. Doc and I. Doc is our private investigator here."

"Okay."

"The reason Elly has been with your husband is because she's using him for his intellectual property and information on studies that he's researching for a new asthma drug. Are you aware of his working on an asthma drug?"

"Yeah. He's been hired by Klinsar, and they're actually releasing the new drug this year. But it's confidential; he'd never share that information with Elly."

"You're right, he's not sharing it. She's stealing it," Bryce said as he reached for a folder. "We have proof that she's gotten hold of classified information down to the details of the ingredients of the drug."

"What?" I asked as he handed me a folder. "What could she possibly want with this information? She won't be able to do anything with it. Eric has patents for all his work."

"That was our first question. She's actually working with her husband and has shared the information with her husband's brother who's one of the senior executives over at Bryner Pharmaceuticals in the UK. Apparently, she and her husband aren't separated, as you thought, but they're still very much married, and he's been making trips back and forth to London."

"Oh my God. I can't believe this. But still, there are patents. They'll never be able to do anything."

Bryce grabbed a tape recorder. "That's where it gets even more devious. We have a recorded conversation of Elly talking to her husband and telling him that she's taken patent forms from Eric's office. We learned that she found where Eric kept his patent-related documents and replaced them with dummy forms. So what he actually mailed out won't protect any of his developments related to the asthma drug. Listen to this, it's fuzzy, you can hear her but not her husband …" He played the recording of Elly.

"Hi … I got them … the patent forms. It was easy; everything is a mess in there. He won't know, but I stuffed the envelopes with plain paper just in case … What? … Okay … Yeah, the patent office won't get anything they can use … I have to go. I'll show you later, Robby … Okay, bye."

I sat there dumbfounded. I couldn't believe this. Elly is one conniving, smart bitch. I couldn't even feel sorry for Eric. How could he be so careless? He'd risked more than he'll ever recover because of lust.

"You there?" Bryce asked.

"Yeah, yeah," I replied. "What a low-down person Elly's brother-in-law is, too, for being a part of this scam."

"That's another thing. We're not even sure that he knows he's getting illegal information. Either he's really good and is doing everything to keep his name clear for when it all goes down, or they've just sold him a bridge."

"Wow," was all that I could say. Then I got a pain in my stomach, so I held it.

"Are you okay?" Bryce asked and stood.

"I'm okay. Sit. I'm okay." I rubbed my stomach. "Okay, Bryce. I need to get out of this marriage now. This is not going to end well, and I don't want to be around when it hits the fan."

"That was going to be my next suggestion. We've been spending a lot of time trying to figure out his assets. Your suspicions were right; he's got them hidden all over the place. But then we stumbled across this new development, and it took our focus. I'll have the divorce papers finalized for you by tomorrow. Question, where is Eric during the day?"

"He's been spending a lot of time in New Jersey, most days and nights actually. Well, he says. He does most of his work at our condo in Hoboken but uses Klinsar's research labs out there from time to time as well. Why?"

"Need to know where to serve him the papers."

"Oh, okay. Oh!" Another major pain in my stomach. Bryce kneeled in front of me.

"What's wrong? What's going on?"

"I don't know. Oh!" More pains.

"Let's get you to the hospital. Do you think you can stand?"

"I can't. I can't."

Bryce opened his office door and called out, "Mara! Call 9-1-1. Pregnant lady in a lot of pain here!"

Next thing I knew, I was on a gurney and then in an ambulance. It was a shame because my hospital is literally only two blocks away from there, so this ride and this traffic were the scenic route for sure. Bryce held my hand in the ambulance.

"My cell phone," I said, pointing to my bag.

He fumbled and dropped everything before managing to locate my cell phone. "Got it."

"Call my doctor. It's number three ... on ... the speed dial. Dr. Green."

"Got it, it's ringing." He put the phone on speaker.

When I heard my doctor say hello, I pointed to my phone then circled my finger in the air—as in "tell him where we are and what's going on."

"Right. Hi ... Yes, this is Bryce Starks, and I'm in an ambulance with Bailey ..."

That's all I remembered hearing. When I came to, I was in a hospital bed with an IV in my arm. I'd call it déjà vu if my stomach was flat and the room was filled with family members. I looked over to my right, and Bryce was sitting in a chair with his eyes closed.

"Bryce. Bryce," I *whispered* loudly.

He opened his eyes quickly and then got up. "Hey, how are you doing?" he asked.

"Much better now. How are *you* doing? I know you don't do hospitals well."

"I am ... okay."

"What happened to me?"

"Your doctor said it was B—Um ... Let me get your doctor."

"Thank you. Hey, did you call anyone else?"

"No, just your doctor."

"Good. Thanks, Bryce."

"No problem."

A minute later, he returned with my doctor.

"How are you feeling?" Dr. Green asked.

"I'm much better. That pain was no joke."

"Yes, you had Braxton Hicks, which are sporadic uterine contractions. They're similar to contractions and are also called *false labor*. It's typical to feel mild cramping."

"There was nothing mild about those."

"You're also very dehydrated. You're going to have to increase your water intake for these remaining weeks. We still have a little ways to go," he said.

"I hope my actual contractions won't be that bad."

My doctor just widened his eyes and grinned. *Great.*

"Can I go home?"

"You can, but you have to promise me that you'll stay in bed. If you get these again, try lying on your left side and don't let your bladder get full. Use the bathroom often."

"More often than I already am?"

"I guess so. This baby is trying to come out a little early, and we just want to wait at least another week. So unless you're using the bathroom or taking a very quick shower, you have to stay in bed."

"I promise. I will," I said. I was so happy that I didn't have to stay overnight, since I'd already had my unfair share of hospital stays.

Olivia met us at my apartment before Bryce took off.

"Thank you for everything, Bryce."

"You're welcome. Make sure you stay in bed," he insisted.

"I will."

"I'll call you tomorrow about the … other thing," he said.

"Yes, please do."

"I like him," Olivia said.

"Yeah?"

"Yeah, he seems like a good one," she added. "Okay, let's go. You're standing too much."

"Yes, ma'am."

WHAT SAY YOU?

The next day I was awoken by my vibrating cell phone on the night stand. I had about twenty text messages and missed calls from Bryce. I got out of bed slowly, so as not to disturb Olivia, and scrolled through the text messages as I walked to the living room. I called Bryce.

"Did you get my messages?" he immediately asked after just one ring.

"Oh my God, Bryce."

"I know. This is crazy. Bryner Pharmaceuticals must have expedited their launch plans to beat Klinsar to the punch."

"Is this confirmed? How did you find out?"

"It started with a tweet from Bryner. I saw it at about two o'clock this morning. And then they announced on their web site that today they were launching *the best thing for asthma sufferers everywhere.*"

"But how? How could they have everything lined up so fast?"

"Doc and I looked over our notes and Elly's activity with her brother-in-law in the UK decreased significantly about

166

three weeks ago. So, I'm thinking they had everything they needed by then. And there was no reason for Klinsar to rush a launch. There was no other competition to their knowledge."

"That makes sense. Wow! Does Klinsar know? Of course they know."

"Oh, yeah. Not only do they know, they've already got their legal team on it. There's a lot of buzz about it in the pharma world all over the Internet. I saw some mention of it at the bottom of the screen on CNN too. This is huge."

"What do you think is going to happen from here?"

"It's hard to say because the launch is in the UK, though patients and doctors anywhere will have access to it. Klinsar can sue, but they likely can't cease what's in progress, which is what they'd need to do to protect their products future and all the projected revenue anticipated from it … wait, there's something about it on the news."

"What channel?"

"It's on CNN."

By the time I got to it, they were onto another topic.

"I missed it," I said. "What did they say?"

"They're already in court. I'm going to see if I can find out what court they're in. They're in New Jersey, so I won't be able to go, but I may be able to send one of the first-years to go. I'll keep you posted. I've gotta run, but I'm emailing over the divorce documents to you this morning to review. We've got to get it in Eric's hands today, if possible."

"Okay."

My head was spinning. Eric must have been grilled by the execs at Klinsar, and I wondered if he'd pieced together the fact that Elly played him. It was weird that he was in the middle of a major scandal—the cause of it—and that it was on the freakin' news. He was not one to admit when he was at fault or *not the hero,* so I was sure that he hadn't fessed up to anything. Knowing him, he was trying to think of a way to cover up that he was the catalyst of this major crime. But, if Elly's husband's brother didn't know that he was getting this data illegally, he was going to turn over names, which would lead straight to Eric. *Right? This is really bad.*

"Hi, Aunt B," Olivia scared and greeted me at the same time. "Sorry."

"Why are you up so early?"

"I didn't see you in bed, so I wanted to check on you."

"I'm fine. Bryce wanted me to see something on TV, that's all. You should go back to bed."

"Okay," she said and then lay on the sofa, with her head in my lap. "What should we have for breakfast?" she asked.

"Ugh. I don't feel like eating anything. I might just do some fruit. But do you want me to make you some blueberry pancakes?"

"Nope."

"You don't want my blueberry pancakes?"

"No cooking. I'll have some cereal," she said, sitting up. "You should go back to bed. It's not sofa-rest; it's bed-rest."

"It's not sofa-rest; it's bed-rest," I mocked. She stood and extended her arm.

"Let's go," she said.

"Fine." Once near the bedroom, my cell phone rang. It was Bryce.

"Go ahead, I'm coming," I said to Olivia. "Hello ... Bryce? I can't hear you; you're breaking up ... What?" *I lost him. Hopefully, he'll text me or something.*

I spent the next few hours looking for updates online, getting pieces of information via text from Bryce and halfway listening to Olivia's stories. The latest I heard from Bryce was that Klinsar was suing Bryner's North American division and attempting to stop the launch of Bryner's version of the asthma drug but were likely not going to be successful at either. By noon London time, the drug had already been released.

I attempted to call Eric, but the call went straight to his voice mail. If I hadn't known what I knew, I'd call, so I figured I'd play the role to keep things *normal.*

I saw an update online stating that Klinsar's team just exited the courtroom. I wondered what that meant. *A break, strategy session, or sign of defeat? Ooh, this baby of mine is kicking today.*

"Are you listening to me, Aunt B?" Olivia asked.

"No," I replied, staring at my computer screen. I felt her looking at me. "Just being honest, sweetie. My mind is on a million things right now. What did you ask me?"

"Is everything okay?"

"I don't know yet." Then she saw my hand on my stomach. "Oh, I'm fine. I just meant ... well, I'm following this news story ... just trying to see what's happening." Then I closed my laptop. "Now what did you ask me?"

"No. I was just saying that I'm going to postpone celebrating my birthday."

"What do you mean? It's this weekend. I thought you were going to Boston with your friends?"

"I'm not going out of town now."

"Why? Because of me?"

She tilted her head to the side.

"No, no, no. It's your eighteenth birthday. You can't stay here because of me."

"I'm not going. I've already canceled it. I'll go next month, after the baby is here."

"Olivia."

"Aunt B. I'm not going. It's fine. I'd be over there calling you every second anyway. How much fun is that?"

I felt guilty. I didn't want her to put off her birthday plans because of me, especially after she'd done so much for me already with the baby shower, getting the baby's room ready, and taking care of me. *Ugh!* I also knew that there was no changing her mind.

Sigh.

"Olivia, Grandma can stay with —"

"No. I'm not going," she interrupted as she flipped through a magazine.

"Okay, how about you and your girlfriends have a slumber party here for your birthday?" *I had her attention.*

"Go on."

"And I can get you a chef to cook whatever you'd like for your birthday dinner. I can also call Sky Spa and get them to send over some people to give you girls manis, pedis, and massages."

"Go on," she said excitedly.

"And I'll ask Grandma to stay with me, so you won't have to worry about me at all," I said. Then she was beaming. "How does that sound?"

"It sounds perfect, Aunt B! Thank you, thank you, thank you!" She gave me a big hug.

"You're welcome, sweetie." Then I held her face and said, "Okay, you call your girls and I'll make some calls to get everything set up."

"Okay!" She jumped off the bed before adding, "You know …"

"Yes?"

"There's this red Gucci handbag that I've had my eye on."

"Reeaallly?"

"Yeesss."

"Spoiler alert."

"Yes?" she said excitedly.

"You're not getting a Gucci bag."

"Aunt B!"

"I already purchased your gift, *and* now you're having a party here with your friends."

"Fine … even though you have a couple of Gucci handbags."

"You make a good point. You know what? When you graduate college, get a good job, and get your first place—"

"Yeah …"

"You can buy yourself one, just like I did." She didn't appreciate that suggestion. But she did finally leave my room after making a face.

I opened up my laptop and refreshed the CNN page for updates on the Eric debacle. *Nothing new.* My cell phone rang. *Bryce.*

"Bryce! What's up?"

"Hey. So, what I've learned is that the judge has denied Klinsar's petition to halt Bryner's launch since, of course, they don't have jurisdiction, and the US subsidiary of Bryner isn't involved or responsible."

"I saw that the attorneys for Klinsar left the courtroom. What was that about?"

"Yeah, they realized they weren't going to get anywhere so they're in 'find out how this happened' mode now so they can start suing somebody."

"Wow ..."

"Yep."

"And Eric?" I asked.

"I don't know where he is actually. I heard that he was in the courtroom, but then he got called out by someone and never returned. I need to find him. Though this may be one of the worst days of his life; unfortunately, it's about to get even worse. I need to have him served with the divorce petition, though the likelihood of him reviewing or signing it right now is slim. And I'm sure Klinsar is going to be up his ass as well for the next few weeks or months even."

"Yeah ..."

"What?"

"Hmm, nothing." It got quiet.

"Are you having second thoughts about divorcing him?"

"No. I'm not having second thoughts at all. I do wish it were already done, though. But it couldn't have been done any sooner than now, so no sense thinking about that. If you find him let me know."

"Okay."

"I mean, after you find him and serve him, let me know."

"Okay. Will do. I'll talk to you soon. And if you happen to hear from him, let me know," he said.

"I will." I tried calling Eric again.

Straight to voice mail. He has to know that I know about this by now. His phone must be turned off. I don't blame him. I'll send him a text message ...

"Aunt B, Carol, Kennedy, Tiffani, and Maria can all make it!" Olivia said excitedly as she re-entered the room.

"Good. And they've asked their parents?"

"Yeah, they have. They're all already eighteen, though. I'm the late one."

"What does being eighteen have to do with asking their parents?"

She thought about it for a few seconds. "Nothing, just saying."

Um hmm. I'm sure they think they're all grown-ups now. Unemployed, degree-less, minor grown-ups.

"You know, we all have our learner's permits, Aunt B," Olivia said, as if she were saying something.

"You know what that means?"

"What?"

"That means that all of you can *walk* wherever you'd like."

"Ha, ha, ha," she said and then put in the earplugs to her iPod.

Several hours passed, and I hadn't heard from Bryce or Eric. I wondered if Eric had turned his phone back on to see my text message. Maybe he was avoiding calls from, well, everyone. I wanted to get to him before he was served with the divorce papers, though. Knowing him, once he was served we'd only be communicating through our attorneys going forward. *Maybe that's for the best actually.* Though his life was crappy right now, I needed a clean break. *He made these choices. He put himself in this situation. I can start the rest of my life right now with just the baby and me.*

Bryce sent a text that said he hadn't located Eric yet. I send Eric another text message, and then I turned off my phone.

BIRTH

By Saturday morning, Olivia and her friends had taken over my living room and most of the other rooms at my place. My mother had been there helping me and allowed me in the living room only for enough time to sing *Happy Birthday* to Olivia the night before and watch her open my gift. It was actually a small Gucci purse. *I couldn't ruin the surprise the other day.* She was thrilled. And then it was back to bed for me. Lisa brought the cake for Olivia and her friends. I was surprised she knew where I lived.

I'd been trying to sleep a lot during those days, though unsuccessfully, because my discomfort was at an all-time high, and Bryce still hadn't located Eric. After I had breakfast, a call came in from a "201" number.

"Hi, is this Mrs. Bryant?"

"Yes. Who's speaking?"

"This is Kirby Niles. I represent Klinsar Limited. Is Eric Bryant available?"

"No, he isn't here."

"He's not there?" He asked as if he were giving me another opportunity to give him the "right" answer.

"No. He isn't here."

"I see." Then he paused as if he were writing or telling someone something. "Be sure to let him know that we're *looking* for him."

"I—" *Click. Dial tone …*

I told Bryce about the call, and then I got a similar call from Klinsar a few hours later, which left me even more unnerved.

I'd finally gotten some sleep, which was surprising given all of the giggles and OMGs coming out of the living room from Olivia and her friends. My phone rang—*at least it's Bryce this time.*

"Hey," I whispered, not wanting to wake my mother. I told her what was going on, minus what Bryce and I knew, behind the scenes—just that the case with Eric's client company and Bryner was happening. It was great to get it off my chest and share it with someone other than Bryce, whom I only had access to in sixty-second increments.

"Hey," he said.

"What's wrong?"

"Klinsar requested proof from the patent office in DC to verify that the asthma drug was indeed theirs, and the patent office confirmed with the judge that no application had been filed with the patent office by Eric or any representative from Klinsar for the drug. I don't think Klinsar has been able to locate Eric ever since that piece of information came in yesterday, which, of course, is why they called you."

Sigh. "I don't know what to think."

"Their calling you could be a cover-up if they actually know where Eric is. I can't tell if he's on the run or if Klinsar's counsel has got him in some secret room somewhere."

"A cover-up for what? If they know where Eric is, why would they want it to appear as if they don't?" I asked.

Bryce didn't respond.

"Bryce?"

"I don't know. Let's not have our minds wander."

"Wander to what, Bryce? What are you thinking?" Whatever he was thinking, I wasn't thinking, and we needed to be on the same page.

"Let me make a few calls and call you back."

"Bryce, stop dodging me. What are you thinking?" I insisted. By now, my mother was fully awake.

"I don't want you to worry —"

"It's too late for that," I snapped.

"He could be corroborating with them and sharing details that they wouldn't want the public to know that he told them. He could be hiding, which wouldn't make a lot of sense because he appears guiltier that way and eventually has to come out of hiding —"

"Or?" I asked. "Or, Bryce? I know how you think, I know there's an *or*."

"Just let me make some calls, okay?" he said softly.

"Okay," I conceded.

"I'll call you as soon as I can. I promise."

"Okay." We hung up.

"What's going on?" my mother asked.

"I'm not sure. No one knows where Eric is, and his client called me looking for him too."

"Really? I'm sure he's fine, honey. He may be talking to his *own* attorney, you know."

"Yeah, you're right. I'm sure everything is okay."

I decided to forgo attempting a nap and took a long warm bath instead, which helped calm my nerves. Mom had fallen back asleep, so I put a blanket over her—then I noticed a missed call and voice mail from an unavailable number. I listened and it was from Eric and he wanted me to meet him somewhere. I felt uneasy when I heard his message. I played it again, and then felt more in control. I knew that if I went to meet Eric that feeling would vanish. I listened to the message one more time, and then I deleted it.

Just one more teenager to go, and I'd have my apartment back to myself. Not that I was allowed to be outside of my bedroom, but at least they'd all be gone, plus it was almost midnight. These girls had school tomorrow, *and* I was tired. Olivia's friend Tiffani was waiting for her aunt to pick her up. I think she just wanted to check my place out and ensure that it was safe.

I wasn't officially a mother yet, but shouldn't adults do that on the front end before I had a chance to sell the child on eBay, spend the money, and relocate?

"She's here," called Olivia from the living room.

"Okay." As I waddled down my hallway, I could see her aunt checking out my stuff and I assumed she was calculating how many coins I must have had to be able to live here with my stuff.

"Hiii! Aww," Tiffani's aunt said in a pitch that made me squint.

"Hi, it's nice to meet you," I said and shook her hand while rubbing my stomach. I assumed the *aww* was in response to my belly and not because I was cute.

I didn't like when strangers touched my stomach, so I put my hand there to prevent her from touching me. *It didn't work.*

"When are you due?" she asked as she rubbed my stomach.

I took a step back and said, "In a week or two."

"You have a gorgeous place," she added and continued her visual tour of the art on my wall. "Is that one by Edvard Munch?"

I wish. She must be just throwing names out there or wants to borrow a lot of money from me. Either way, I'm too pregnant and tired for this conversation.

"No, it's not," I said.

"I feel like I've been here before," she said.

"I don't think so. We've been here some time and are the original owners."

"We?" she asked.

"Yes, my husband Eric and I."

"Oh," she replied, brows raised as if *now it all made sense.* "Tiffani, let's go." She couldn't have exited my place any quicker.

What the hell was that about?

Then I was wide awake, so Olivia and I shared a bowl of my favorite organic kettle-corn popcorn. I had a cup of orange juice too; it was my preferred combination of treats at the time.

"Oh, Tiffani said that she left her shoes here," Olivia said while looking at her phone.

"You can get them to her tomorrow, right?" I asked very quickly. *No need having guests again tonight.*

"Yes, Aunt B," Olivia replied knowing exactly why I asked.

My phone rang. *Bryce, calling pretty late.*

"Hello … Bryce?" I said and then looked at my phone. I only heard static. *He needs a new provider.* "Bryce?" The call dropped. He called back. "Hello," I said and waited for a response. *Nothing.* Now a little static and then the call dropped again. This happened about five more times. By now my bowl of popcorn was empty, and I had gotten tired. I yawned—nice and loud and deep.

"Uh, ready for bed?" Olivia asked sarcastically.

"I am." By the time I changed into my pajamas, Olivia was already in the bed with her eyes closed. *Do I move that slowly?* She looked like she was already on her second dream.

I got into bed, and just when I was about to turn the light out on the nightstand, there was a knock at my door. Olivia popped up, and we looked at each other.

"I know she didn't come by just to get her shoes, Olivia," I said, totally annoyed.

Olivia shrugged. "I don't—I thought she was going to just get them from me tomorrow."

Sigh.

I got out of bed and went to the door. *How did they get upstairs without the doorman calling anyway?* I looked through the peephole and froze. Then I opened the door. Two police officers were standing in front of me.

"We're so sorry to disturb you ma'am. Are you Mrs. Bryant?" one of them asked and removed his cap. I nodded and stared at him, my mind going to bad places.

Then the other officer pulled a photo out of his chest pocket, showed it to me, I stopped breathing and he asked, "Is this your husband, Eric Bryant?" I nodded again, and then he looked at the other officer.

Nothing was said for three seconds that felt like twenty minutes. Then one of them finally said, "We regret to inform you that ..." That's all I heard before I fell to my knees and screamed. I saw Olivia running down the hallway to me in my peripheral, and then she was holding me. Then one of the officers was kneeling down in front of me ... or maybe both of them. And then I heard my cell phone ringing again from my bedroom. That's all that I remember.

DEATH

It was five-thirty in the morning, and everyone was at my apartment. My parents were there, my brothers, my sister, Aunt Janet, Eric's brother Scott, and Bryce. I was lying on the sofa with a cool towel on my head, my legs propped on pillows and my mother rubbing my arm. Some were sitting, some were standing, and some were pacing. I could feel each of them staring at me at one point or another. My eyes were on the ceiling.

The family was in shock, especially my mother who was trying to hold it together. I kept replaying things in my head, but I kept getting interrupted with other irrelevant thoughts or a family member who was bad at whispering. I needed to get Bryce alone. By the time he arrived, Dad also had just arrived, so I couldn't ask him anything. And then more people came, which made it impossible to speak with him privately. We kept giving each other these looks like, "I wish everyone would leave so that we could talk."

My home phone rang and Dad answered it right when Scott was about to reach for it. They've both been intercepting calls for the past couple of hours, mainly from the police and FBI who'd finally left thirty minutes prior.

"Hello … Who's calling?" he asked. Dad sighed and said, "Okay, hold on." He handed me the phone. "It's the police again. He says he just has a quick question."

"Yes?" I answered.

"Mrs. Bryant. Sorry to disturb you again during this difficult time," said the officer.

"It's okay."

"Just a quick question. Did you communicate with Eric at all in the last twenty-four hours? We understand that you hadn't seen him, but did you hear from him?"

ACTL …"No. I hadn't."

"Okay. Thank you, Mrs. Bryant. Again, we're very sorry."

"Yeah."

"Let me talk to them," said Scott.

I handed him the phone and lay back down. *That was only the beginning. The days to come were filled with calls, updates, and questions from the cops.*

"You should eat something, honey," Mom said.

I shook my head. I heard my sister in the kitchen, probably making coffee. I wanted everyone to leave. I appreciated the gesture, but their presence wasn't helping me right now. I needed to speak with Bryce. I was numb.

I sent Bryce a text message and asked him to go hang out at the corner coffee shop, so I could get my family out of here without them wondering why he was staying behind.

Unfortunately, my eyes had closed—and for too long. My living room was empty, so I sat up then heard voices in the kitchen. *Damn, they're still here.* I looked at the cable box. Nine o'clock. *Damn.* Bryce must be long gone by now. Olivia entered the living room.

"Aunt B," she said somberly and sat next to me.

"Hi, sweetie." She held my arm, and I rubbed hers. "Who's still here?" I asked.

"Everybody."

"Olivia, I want everybody to go home. Can you make that happen for me, please?"

"Yes. I'll do it." Then she walked straight into the kitchen like a soldier on a mission.

I headed to my bedroom, and Mom entered shortly after with watery eyes. I patted my bed.

"Mom—"

"You shouldn't be here without me, honey," she said trying to hold back tears. *She's going to make me cry.* I just held her, then wiped the tears off her face.

"We cooked all types of food. What can I get for you?" Mom asked and caressed my face. *If I didn't let her feed me, she would have no peace.*

"I'll eat in a minute."

"I can't imagine how you're feeling right now."

"However I'm supposed to feel, you know, given the circumstances, I don't."

"I know it's hard."

"There was a lot going on before ... Eric's death."

"We don't know that he's dead."

"Mom."

"Until a body is found, we can't say," she said.

"Mom, his car was found by—"

She raised her hand not wanting to hear more. Then she said, "What did you mean there was a lot going on?"

And then Olivia walked into my room with a tray of food, so I ate some then looked back at Mom.

"I learned that Eric was unfaithful to me not too long ago, Mom."

Her eyes widened.

"Eric?" she asked in disbelief and then she looked at Olivia briefly, who didn't make eye contact with her.

"Yeah, Eric. I won't go into all of the details, but up until the last few hours, I … I had planned to divorce him."

"Oh my goodness," she said. This was too much for her to process so I left it at that for now. *It stayed quiet for a bit.*

"I need to speak with my friend, Bryce. He's an attorney, and he may have some information for me on what happened leading up to yesterday. He followed the situation with Eric's client and the other pharmaceutical company, so I really want to talk with him."

"Okay, yeah you should talk to him," Mom said.

"I'm going to ask him to come over. But I need to speak with him privately, okay?"

"Sure, of course."

There was a knock on the front door then Mom left and Olivia escorted Bryce to my room.

"I actually brought them both up-to-speed on Eric, the basics anyway. That's how I got them to give us time to chat," I said.

"Ah, okay. I was surprised when they opened the door and even more surprised when they didn't ask me any questions. Makes sense now."

I nodded. "So what have you been able to find out?"

Bryce sighed like he had more data than his brain could handle. "Well, Eric's car was found on the GW bridge, as you know. And um ..."

"It's okay, Bryce. I'm okay. Just tell me everything."

"They're still searching for a body but are prematurely classifying it as a suicide."

"I know, but he would never kill himself. No matter how bad it got, he wouldn't do that."

Bryce paused before saying, "A suicide note was found."

"I know but ... I just don't believe he'd do that."

"The note was typed, but it had Eric's signature on it. And the signature matched his."

"I didn't know that. They're not sharing all the details with me."

"In the note he mentioned being fired by Klinsar for unlawful activity that he wasn't guilty of, and he talked about the impact it would have on his reputation forever, and he mentioned being set up."

"It said all of that?"

"Yeah," Bryce said. Then we were both quiet. "So you think he's still alive?"

"No."

"Oh. I thought—"

"I just don't think he killed himself."

"What do you think happened?"

I shook my head. "What do you think happened?" I asked him.

Bryce just looked at me.

"Say it," I said.

A CHANCE TO LIE

"I think … he killed himself, but you know him better than me."

I just looked at him.

"I'm sorry," he said.

"I know." He took my hand. "We have a lot of evidence, Bryce."

"I know. I wanted to talk to you about that too."

"We should turn it over to the police or FBI, right?"

"I think there are still some unknowns and we should turn in the evidence, but not yet. Those calls that you got from Klinsar's counsel … that wasn't cool."

"Yeah, that didn't sit well with me at all."

"I know. And that's part of what makes me say we should wait it out and see what transpires in the coming weeks before speaking with anyone. Your safety is the most important thing."

"You're right. Not yet."

"Okay."

"Were you ever able to serve Eric with the divorce papers?" I asked.

"No."

"Who knows that I planned to divorce him?"

"Nobody."

"No one at all?"

"No one at all. My investigator knew that we were looking into him but not that you planned on divorcing Eric."

"What about the courts? Didn't you have to file something with the court?"

"No. I drew up the petition that you reviewed and was going to serve him with it. It didn't get to the court stage yet. That would've been afterwards, if he objected."

"Oh," I said.

"Why?"

I didn't respond.

"What?" he asked.

"Everyone would think I was the most horrible person right now, if they knew."

LIFE AFTER DEATH

A week later, my apartment looked like the New York Botanical Gardens. There were flowers of all sorts throughout the living room, dining room, and foyer. Everyone that I knew and hardly knew had sent me sympathy flowers, cards, and balloons to express their condolences. I had to turn the ringer on my home phone off because the calls were too much. The flowers were very thoughtful, but the upkeep of all the foliage was becoming a part-time job ... for Olivia. I was still on bed-rest, so I was doing less than nothing while she was doing pretty much everything. I promised her that when the baby came and things calmed down, I'd make it up to her.

I had another week to go until my due date and asked my doctor if it'd be okay if the baby came now, right now. He said it would be okay if the baby *naturally* came now, but there was no medical need to induce labor. Surely being tired as hell, the inability to see my feet or get through an hour or a knock-knock joke without peeing a little—surely this was a medical need. I was determined to give birth on *this very day*.

And I had that same conversation with myself … for the next three weeks.

Now this baby was almost two weeks overdue, and I wasn't sure if it was the series of hostile messages I left my doctor or a medical need at this point but I was officially scheduled for a C-section at four o'clock.

"Let's take your mind off the belly, Aunt B. Want to help me pick out a dress for Maria's party?"

"Sure, whatcha got?" Olivia ran to the bedroom and came back modeling a fuchsia cocktail dress.

She stood with her hands on her hips and said, "What do you think?"

I tilted my head to the right and said, "I'm not loving this one. The color is great, but the design is blah."

"Really?" I nodded. "Okay, I have another one," and she ran off to the bedroom. When she returned, she was wearing a more fitted jade green sheath dress. "What about this one?" she asked with a big grin. I tilted my head to the right and then to the left. "Isn't it better than the other one?"

"Well … it's less worse than the other one."

"Aunt B!"

"What? You want the truth, right?"

"Yeah, but you told me that jade was my color."

"The color is perfect on you, but the style is an enemy to my eyes." She shook her head and then I grabbed my stomach.

"What? Are you okay?" she asked and ran to my side.

I looked her in the eye and said, "Olivia, it's time."

"It's time — It's time-time?"

"It's time-time. The hideous jade dress did it."

Olivia laughed and then she got real serious. "Okay, I'll grab your hospital bag. Let me call Jack to hail a taxi for us. Call Grandma and Grandpa, right?"

"Yes," I said and tried to stand up.

"Wait, don't get up until we're ready to go. Let me make the calls."

"But I'm wet." I leaned my head back on the sofa to take a deep breath. Finally, when I take control and schedule a C-section, this offspring of mine reminds me who's still in charge. The pain subsided, but my expensive sofa was now absorbing my fluids. *Yeah, this isn't good.* I stood up, and Olivia signaled for me to sit down while she was on the phone. I took the cover off of the sofa cushion, and luckily it hadn't soaked through yet. *Yay!* I waddled to my bathroom and thoroughly rinsed the sofa cushion in my sink. I know my focus was in the wrong place, but why spend thousands on a new sofa if I can save this one? I hung the cover over the bathtub to dry — and just in time.

"What are you doing?"

"Okay, okay. I'm done. Now I just need to change." She shooed me out of the bathroom. "As soon as that cushion cover is dry," I said. "Could you take it to the cleaners downstairs for me, please?"

"Yes, yes. Let's go, the taxi is on its way." I changed clothes and then the nerves kicked in.

When I got to the hospital, I was wheeled to my room where my parents were already waiting.

"How many traffic laws did you break to get here?" I asked.

Dad said, "None. We were on our way to you when Olivia called."

"Oh, okay." I only partially believed him. I climbed into the bed.

"How do you feel?" Mom asked.

"Excited, nervous, and super uncomfortable … Ow! For sure … Ooh!"

The nurse walked in in the midst of my *ows* and *oohs*, so she checked out what was happening under my sheet then promptly said, "Okay, Bailey. It's show time."

"Bye, Dad," I said immediately.

Dad said, "I know. Okay. Love you, honey," before Mom scooted him out of the room. The doctor entered, and it was show time indeed.

"Hi, Bailey," said Dr. Green. "Are you ready to do this?"

"Oohhhhh!!!" I screamed in absolute pain. *What the hell did I get myself into here?* Olivia took my hand. *Poor girl.* I hoped I hadn't crushed her fingers. Mom alternated between wiping my face, fanning me, and checking on the progress of my baby. Wow … *my* baby. *This is really happening.*

"You're doing great, Bailey," said Dr. Green.

"I see the head," said Mom.

"Really?" Olivia said and attempted to go look, but I wouldn't let her hand go. "I can see it later."

"Whoa!" I screamed.

"Nice one, Bailey," said the doctor. "We've got the shoulders. Good job! This baby is anxious to come out."

192

"Everything is looking good," said the nurse, whose gentle voice gave me comfort.

"Aunt B, it's happening. You're about to be a mom," said Olivia.

"Yeah. I am ... Oh my goodness." I thought back to when Olivia was born and how she, too, was ready to come out quickly. And now she stood here holding *my* hand. And that the next time I walked into my apartment, I'd have a baby with me.

"Ohhhh!!" *Okay, that one really hurt.*

"Come on, honey. You've got this," said Mom. Dad must've been pacing in the waiting area and eating M&Ms as he had when all of my nieces and nephews entered the world.

"One more push and we're there," said Dr. Green.

Really? Don't get me wrong, this was the worst pain imaginable, and I'd give anything to end it — but I assumed I'd be like this for more than ten minutes. *One more push it is.*

"Aaahhhh!!!" I screamed and gave an award-winning push. And then it was like I had completed the biggest bowel movement ever — with some dangling parting gifts. *Sorry.* The pain was almost entirely gone, or maybe I was just imagining that it was because everyone was quiet.

"Oh my," said Dr. Green.

"What, oh my?" I asked. Then my mother was freaking me out as she stood still next to the doctor with her mouth open, not blinking or breathing.

"Oops," said the doctor, amused.

"Oops? What oops?" I asked.

"You want to tell her?" said the doctor to Mom.

"It's a girl, honey," said Mom.

I gasped. I think I was holding my breath all that time waiting for them to say something. "It's a girl, honey" echoed in my head over and over.

"What?" I asked.

"A girl," said Dr. Green. "I ... that sonogram was fuzzier than I thought. Must've gotten a scan of the cord and thought it was ... anyway, you have a girl." Olivia and I looked at each other.

"I want to see her," I said, as if I didn't believe them. And I finally released Olivia's hand.

"Let's get her cleaned up. Who's going to cut the umbilical cord?" Dr. Green asked.

"Me!" Mom said then looked at me.

"Go ahead, Mom. You do the honors." The doctor handed Mom the surgical scissors and showed her where to cut. She was so excited. *It was so cute.*

"I've never gotten to do this before," she said. Then she exhaled and pointed to the spot the doctor showed her. He nodded and then my mother cut the cord. They wiped my baby up and weighed her.

"Seven pounds, eleven ounces," the nurse said.

I could hardly wait to hold her. They wrapped her in a blanket, put a cap on her, and placed her in my arms.

"Oh my God." I could spend the rest of my life right here just holding her and staring into her eyes. *I was so in love.* Today was Day One of the beginning of my life. Olivia joined me in gawking over this tiny precious piece of joy.

"Aunt B ... She's so beautiful. It's a girl. It's a girl!" she said excitedly, seeming to just realize what had transpired. Mom walked up to the head of my bed and realized the impact of this moment—that I was now a mom too. She stared, along with Olivia and me. The room was quiet. *And I was exhausted.*

"Mom, get Dad."

"Um, hmm," she replied and didn't move an inch.

"I'll get him," the nurse said.

"Thank you."

Dad walked into the room all smiles as he stood next to Mom.

"What do we have here?" he whispered.

"A beautiful little girl, Dad."

"A girl?" he asked in shock. "Ha ha!" he clapped his hands loudly. The baby jerked a bit.

"Dad, you startled her."

Mom elbowed him.

"Sorry, sorry," he whispered. "Are you allowing anyone to hold her?"

"Umm hmm … tomorrow," I replied, not even looking up from her.

"So have we thought of a name for this little angel?" Dr. Green asked.

I looked up with wide eyes at Olivia and then at my parents.

"I haven't even thought of any girl's names. Oh my gosh. I was focused on boy's names," I said. "Olivia, what should we name her?"

Olivia looked at me and said, "Umm … Let's name her Jade."

"Jade?" I asked and chuckled, and Olivia nodded. "Okay," I said and then looked at my doctor. "Her name is Jade Morgan Bryant."

"Aww ..." my parents said in unison. *They spend way too much time together.*

"You'll look out for her always, right Olivia?"

"Always."

"You look tired but would you like to try breastfeeding Jade now?" Dr. Green asked.

"Yes, definitely," I replied. "Bye, Dad."

"It's okay," he said and headed toward the door. "I'll go and buy something for my granddaughter downstairs."

"Barney's is right up the street," Olivia said.

"Aww, you're looking out for Jade already," I replied.

"But of course," she replied. "Plus, I'm *also* a granddaughter."

"There it is," I said.

A few hours later, I woke from a nap and my parents were sitting in the corner of my room chatting. Then Scott appeared in the doorway.

"Scott."

"Hey. I've been calling you all day. Now I see why I kept getting your voice mail."

"Is everything okay?" Mom asked.

Scott looked at her then looked at me.

"I shouldn't have come," he said.

Dad stood up and said, "What's going on?"

Scott looked at me and then signaled to Dad to go out into the hall with him.

"No, no, no," I said, and sat up. "What's going on, Scott?"

Scott sighed and said, "The police have been trying to reach you all day. When they couldn't reach you they called me, then I kept calling you and—"

"Why?" I asked.

Scott looked at the floor. My dad put his hand on Scott's shoulder, and said, "It's okay, son."

"The um ... police wanted you to ... They want you to go and identify a body they found. They think it might be—" And then he broke down and cried. Dad consoled him. Mom and I just looked at each other.

"Will you go?" I asked Scott.

He looked at me, and then he nodded.

NEXT UP

I'd been having a lot of dreams about Eric. And in every dream, I didn't have a voice. I'd try to speak, but no words came out. I'd see him walking toward dangerous rooms that had angry FBI agents with weapons, or Elly in a room filled with fire, and I tried to warn him, but he couldn't hear me. I couldn't even hear myself. I talked to my parents about it, and they said maybe it was because I didn't have closure. I didn't confront him about the cheating; he didn't know that I wanted the divorce, and then—Bam! He was in the midst of all the legal trouble. I felt cheated ... again. With everything, though, I hadn't cried at all.

Scott called me a few hours after he visited me at the hospital.

"Bailey."

Since he called versus stopping by, I assumed everything was okay.

"Hey, did—"

"We need to plan the funeral."

Just like that. No pause, no emotion, no room for questions. His words were an immediate shock to my system. I'd convinced myself that Eric was dead because that was better than hating him alive. But actually hearing it ...

"Okay," I said.

"I'll take care of —"

"No. I'll do it."

Eric's funeral was short and sweet—just thirty minutes long. We had it at the church he and I joined when we first got married. I got to the church before any guests, sat and reminisced about those early years when we attended church regularly. Eric and I were active members, and he was more humble then. I wonder how our marriage would have ended up if we continued to go to church. *Why did we even stop going in the first place?* I wanted to keep the funeral small, so I only invited my family, Scott (Eric's parents had died when he was young), Christina, and her husband, Eric's colleagues and peers in the industry, and a few neighbors of ours. Scott insisted that the casket be closed. According to him, the condition of Eric's body wouldn't have been easy on the eyes. So we displayed a large portrait of Eric in front of the sanctuary.

At the end, I thanked everyone for coming and invited them for refreshments downstairs, but I immediately left. Surprisingly, my sisters left with me. They'd actually been supportive lately, but it was weird since we'd been estranged for so long. My sister, Tina, had been Skyping from Pennsylvania with Jade and me. She also stayed with me the entire weekend of the funeral and did all of the cooking. Lisa called and stopped by every other day after work and brought Jade tons of pink baby clothes, since everything I had was gender-neutral or blue. Her stopping by only lasted two weeks, but she'd still call.

There was a criminal investigation underway against Elly and her husband, Robby. Bryce and I continued to follow the case and were prepared to share our evidence with the FBI if it looked like either of them were going to get off. I'd gotten obsessed with monitoring the details and updates of the case so I decided that I needed to pull back and focus on my new baby at home. I asked Bryce to keep me informed of the major highlights and turning points, and he did.

I hadn't followed up with any of the nannies I'd interviewed a couple of months back. My parents were with me now, but Mom only agreed to grand-nanny part-time; Olivia had school, so she'd be here in the evening, but I wanted her focused on her senior-year activities. And I planned to return to work when the baby was about two or three months old.

My parents ended up helping me go through and select the perfect nanny—Edna, who was highly recommended by Christina. *What would I do without them all?*

I walked into the living room, where my mother hovered over Jade who was asleep in her bassinet.

"A watched pot never boils, mother." She raised her hands and followed me into the kitchen.

"I'm making eggplant Parmesan with angel hair pasta. The way you like it," said Dad.

"Delish. Count me in." He made great eggplant Parmesan.

Olivia walked into the kitchen and made a face when she saw the eggplant.

"What are you going to eat then?" I asked her.

"I don't know. Maybe I'll make something," she said. My mother and I didn't look at each other, but I was sure we both had the same *please don't cook* expression.

"Well, Grandpa is making pasta too, so just have pasta and sauce," I suggested.

"But the sauce doesn't have any meat in it, right?" she asked Dad.

"No. No meat in this one. Sorry," he said.

"I'll do that then! I'll make a meat sauce. Aunt B, we have ground beef, right?" Olivia asked.

"How would she know?" my mother joked.

"Hey, I cook … too. Sometimes … Right?" I asked. The quiet was my answer. I guess I hadn't cooked in a while. "Well, I know that we definitely have ground beef," I added. "Probably …" I checked the fridge.

My mother shook her head and said, "Olivia, I can make you some meat sauce with some of Grandpa's sauce."

"I can do it Grandma," Olivia said. It was exactly what we didn't want her to say. "I'll wait until Grandpa's finished, so I can have the kitchen to myself."

"I'm done. All yours," he said.

"Thanks!" Olivia replied, then shooed us all out of the kitchen.

"We're going, we're going," I said and made my way over to Jade who was tossing in her bassinet. My mother was right behind me—directly behind me. *My shadow.* Anytime I headed toward Jade, she tried to get there first. When I knew

Jade had a bunch of yuck in her diaper, I'd trick Mom and act like I was going for Jade. Then she'd beat me to it, but I ended up the real winner. I think I'd only changed one number two in the past three weeks. *Like how I did that?*

My mother and I looked at each other and agreed that Jade wasn't ready to be up just yet. Actually, I said it and then she went and checked anyway. It was funny but annoying at times because she did that for all of my Jade observations and decisions. So I took a seat on the sofa, and Mom did too, but she made sure that she was closer in proximity to Jade. *She's a mess.*

We all chatted for a bit and then I said, "Okay, question. Who is going to eat some of Olivia's pasta sauce?" *Silence.* "Come on. If none of us at least taste it, she's going to feel bad," I said. *More silence.* "Okay, whoever tastes her sauce gets unlimited time with Jade tonight," I propositioned. They both sat up in their seats.

"Unlimited?" Mom asked.

"Yep."

"And we don't have to share that time with anyone else?" Dad asked.

"That's correct."

"Deal," said Dad.

"Deal," said Mom.

"Good," I said. "Now if you end up spending most of the night over the toilet, you cannot take my baby in there with you." Mom waved her hand.

Olivia walked into the living room. "I'll set the table," she said then headed back to the dining room.

"Your sauce isn't ready already, is it?" I asked.

"Um hmm," Olivia replied.

"Yeah, you cannot take my baby into the bathroom with you," I whispered again to my parents, and they shook their heads.

We made our way to the dining room while Olivia and Dad brought the food out to the table. Olivia brought her *special* meat sauce out last in a serving bowl. It smelled all the way wrong.

"Olivia. Sweetie," I said as I dug a serving spoon into her creation and stirred it a bit, "Is this meat fully cooked?"

"I cooked it for eight minutes; that's how long my mom cooks her meatballs for," Olivia replied.

"Your meatballs look bigger than the ones your mom usually makes," Mom said.

"Hmm … how exactly did you prepare your meat sauce?" I asked. *Something just wasn't right.*

"I rolled up the ground beef into balls, put seasoning on them, and I put some of Grandpa's sauce in a pot. Then I put the meatballs in the sauce for eight minutes on low heat," Olivia said innocently.

"Oh!" Dad said.

"Oh, wow," Mom added.

"What?" Olivia asked not understanding the concern.

"Yeah, sweetie … this is not FDA-approved," I said. Mom tried to hide her sounds but was unsuccessful. Olivia stirred her creation and looked defeated.

"It's okay," I went on. "It was your first attempt. But you were supposed to fully cook the meatballs separately and then add them to the sauce. This isn't cooked, sweetie. And it's probably not safe to eat." She was so disappointed.

"Okay," she said sadly and picked up her dish from the table. My parents and I watched her walk away.

"Olivia," I said, and she turned around, "Let's make a new meat sauce together."

"Really? But everyone is about to eat," she replied.

"It's okay. You guys go ahead and eat." Then Olivia and I headed into the kitchen; she was excited now. Luckily, since Dad had cooked in the army, he cooked as if food grew on trees, *ha ha*, so there was still plenty of pasta sauce left. I showed Olivia how to sauté onions and peppers, season the ground beef and simmer it all in a pan. As it cooked, she noticed how the aroma smelled quite differently than hers did. I let her drain the meat and add it to the sauce. I shared my healthy cooking tips with her, like browning the meat in water instead of oil and using fresh herbs and seasonings. I forgot how much I enjoyed cooking.

"Bailey, your phone is ringing. It's Bryce," said my mom. *Who needs Caller ID when you have an inquisitive mother?*

"Thanks," I said and got the phone. "Hey, guess what I'm making?"

"What?" Bryce asked.

"Olivia and I are making meatballs." Bryce loved meatballs.

"Oh yeah? Are you boasting or offering?"

"Boasting."

"Ouch." I laughed.

"Just kidding," I said. "Would you like some?"

"Is the whole family over?"

"Yeah, kinda."

"That's okay, maybe another time. Feel free to put a few aside for me though."

"Will do. When's the last time you cooked, Bryce?"

"I just cooked some noodles yesterday."

"Are you trying to get credit for making noodles?"

"Well … not anymore."

"Thank you."

"It's all ready, Aunt B," said Olivia.

"I'll let you go," said Bryce.

"Okay, talk to — wait, did you call for something?"

"No, just calling."

"Oh, okay."

Olivia was on her third tasting of our masterpiece.

"Save some for the pasta, Olivia," I joked. Then I took a spoonful of the sauce and walked back into the dining room where my parents were eating.

"Hey," I said, and they looked up at me with mouths full of food. And then I ate a spoonful of the meat-sauce and said, "Guess who gets unlimited time with Jade tonight?" Then I winked at them and walked away before they had time to swallow and protest. *I should have been an attorney; there's always fine print with me.*

I'd been enjoying motherhood. It was not what I'd expected. I'd gotten myself all nervous for nothing. If I were to complain about anything, which I won't — except for right now, it'd be that my Mom, who was super helpful, had … taken over. If I bathed Jade then put her PJ's on, Mom would "evaluate" her and Jade would end up with different PJ's come bedtime. It started with little things but got to the point where she'd take Jade out of my arms and would finish whatever I'd been in process of doing. I should've said something. *Ugh.*

We celebrated our first Christmas with Jade, and things were so different from the previous year when I had been in the car accident, and my family hadn't known if I was going to make it.

Even though Mom had been overbearing, I had special moments with Jade every day and it was so awesome. The way she looked back at me, made me forget everything negative that had transpired. *I loved her so much.* I could stare into her eyes all day, but if I didn't get back to work soon we'd all have to live on my breast milk, and Mom would have to give up that expensive maple syrup that she couldn't live without.

I didn't miss work necessarily, but I did miss the conversations, my office, lunches with Christina—everything that wasn't in my job description. So, I looked forward to those things being a part of my life again. What I didn't look forward to was seeing Dennis. *Ugh.* What a disappointment. I learned that he told Stephen the job was his right after I got on board with the LA project. He knew long before it was announced that I wasn't getting the promotion, but he wanted Gwen Stefani; then he let me work like a dog and got all the great ideas out of me only to hand them and the opportunity over to Stephen—who, I heard, was failing miserably. What a shame. Anyway, it is what it is. *I loathe that adage, but it's always so applicable* ... Two to three months turned into six months, but I finally decided to go back to work.

THE OFFICE

When I went back to work, I received the weirdest mixed greetings. They were a combination of congratulations and sad faces, then it hit me—I had a husband the last time I was here. *They're reacting to the news of both Jade and Eric. What's wrong with me? How did I forget that? If I've forgotten it at all, I am my parent's child—pink elephant ignorer.* And my family didn't talk about it at all, ever. I didn't know if that was the right thing to do or not, but it had been all about Jade, Olivia, and the other kids—all the good stuff. *It's been great, but is it normal?* It felt genuine, but was I dodging an emotional breakdown? I had been so mad at Eric, and then that anger was abruptly paused, and then it just got placed, rather misplaced, into a cloud, one of those clouds where people place their files and other documents—and Olivia places her photos, to retrieve at a later date … *I just hope I get to choose the date. I hope I'm not on the subway one day and just lose it. Those scenarios tend to end up on YouTube.*

Christina and I were chatting in my office when Dennis walked by. Then he walked into my office.

"Good morning, ladies," he said. "It's great to have you back."

"Hey, Dennis," said Christina.

"Dennis," I replied. "It's nice to be back." And then there was silence.

"Well, I have a meeting in a few minutes. I'll stop by later," Christina said. I gave her a "please don't leave" look that she completely ignored.

"So how have you been?" he asked me.

"Just fine," I said curtly.

"I'm so sorry about your husband." I just nodded. "But you look great, and you have a beautiful little girl. Congratulations. Christina showed us some photos. She looks just like you." I nodded again. "I sent you flowers. Did you get the flowers?"

"Yes, I got all of the flowers." We just looked at each other.

"Look, I didn't know what to—"

"How's Stephen doing in his new senior manager role?"

Dennis just stared at me because surely I knew that Stephen was as successful as a floppy-disk salesman in Silicon Valley.

"I'll let you get to work. I'm sure you have a lot to catch up on," Dennis said and headed for the door. "Welcome back." *Whatever, president of the damn "Boys Club."*

After all the years of working together, I'd hoped that by now he'd see my value. Stephen hadn't been there half the time that I had, and he'd had so many complaints brought against him, yet he got the promotion. *Thank God for Jade. She is what I am now fully focused on, not this place.*

By the end of the week, I was pretty much back into the swing of things. Christina, Bryce, and I planned to have lunch, but she had a meeting run over so she asked me to go ahead and she'd meet us there. As I headed across the street, Bryce texted and said he was ten minutes behind. *Am I the only one who knows that it's Friday?* Since I had a few minutes, I stopped by a shoe boutique before going to the restaurant. Bryce was there by the time I got there.

"I thought you were ten minutes behind?" I asked.

"I was. You're just getting here?"

"Yeah, I stopped by Stuart Weitzman's since you two were running late. Guess who I saw?"

"Who? Wait, what'd you buy?"

"Me, nothing."

"No shoes stuffed in that huge purse?"

"Nope."

"Okay, are there unicorns in this fiction story?"

"What? No! This is a true story. I can enter a shoe store and not buy anything, Bryce."

"Okay," he said. "So, they didn't have your size?"

"Ha ha. Anyway, I just saw P. Diddy across the street."

"Yeah, he was at my office a few minutes ago."

"He was?"

"Yeah. You didn't purchase any shoes, Diddy was just in my office, and Christina is back there in the restroom."

"Christina is in the bathroom?"

"You didn't notice the common theme in my sentence?" I hit his arm.

"Where is she anyway?" Just then, both of our phones beeped. Christina sent text messages that said to proceed without her.

"Alrighty then."

"Long Friday meetings suck. I'll bring her something back."

"Aren't you sweet?"

"You're paying, but I'll take that," I said and winked.

"Are you flirting with me?"

"Uh, no."

"Oh."

"Seeing Mr. Combs reminded me of when I wanted to pursue a singing career back in high school."

"Oh gosh."

"I'm serious! I was a pretty good singer."

"I was a pretty good Batman in seventh grade, too."

I laughed. "I can't stand you."

"You think you've still got it?" he asked.

"I'm sure I could belt a note that would impress even you. If I put together a demo tape, would you share it with one of your celebrity producer clients?"

"Let's cross that imaginary bridge when we get to it."

We had a manager's meeting scheduled that afternoon, and I planned to head out right afterwards. Minutes before the meeting, I got a phone call, and, after I hung up, I hadn't even noticed Christina standing in my office doorway.

"Hellooo," she said. "Are you okay?"

"What? Yeah, I'm fine."

"Your mind is totally somewhere else. Who was that?"

"Oh that was just ... an acquaintance calling from Canada."

"Oh. Sure you're okay?"

"Yeah, we should probably head to the meeting."

We walked into the conference room, and the table was filled with pastries. *Who started this foolishness? Ugh! I'm four pounds away from my pre-pregnancy weight—no temptations!* Dennis was ready to begin the meeting and was apparently in a good mood. Stephen wasn't present, which was unfortunate. I was eager to hear how things had been going with his new role—from *his perspective.*

"All right team, let's get started," Dennis began. "I have some news to share. Today was Stephen Murray's last day with knirD."

What? Christina and I looked at each other in shock—this must have just happened.

Dennis continued. "We parted on good terms, and he has some exciting opportunities ahead of him." *Yeah right.* "But," he continued, "this shift couldn't have happened at a better time. Another trailblazer; the right person, in fact, is back just in time to replace Stephen and do what he didn't get a chance to accomplish." *Didn't get a chance to accomplish or couldn't accomplish? What a joke. Why is Dennis looking at me? Now why is everyone starting to look at me? Are you kidding me? He wants me to take the senior manager role now, as the damn Plan B person?* I looked at Dennis, and he smiled and looked at me waiting for a response.

I grabbed my tablet and left the room, slamming the door behind me.

How's that for an answer, you prick?

I headed back to my office and slammed that door too, before I paced my office fuming. He hadn't even discussed this with me first. *How disrespectful! He just mentions it in front of everyone as if I'm going to cave to the moment and say yes.* I thought I couldn't dislike him any more than I already did. I was even ready to put my angry feelings toward him aside and just get on with business—and he pulled this? *What a horrible boss! That was his most ridiculous stunt to date!* For all I knew, Stephen could have quit, and Dennis just wanted me to fill the vacancy before his own boss got on his case. I'd never felt so underappreciated and insulted in all my time here.

Christina walked into my office and said, "Wow!"

"Can you believe he pulled that mess?" I said.

"I can't believe he just did that. Did he really think you'd accept it that way?"

"Right! What VP does that? What … what the hell is wrong with him? I am so angry. I knew I was more qualified for that damn job than Stephen, and he knew it too! Now he offers me the second-place prize, the runner-up opportunity of a lifetime? He can kick rocks!"

Then Christina and I laughed. "Kick rocks" was her phrase of choice for a former employee she detested. She used to say it all the time until the person left the company. We hadn't heard it in a while.

I slumped in my chair, and she sat across from me. "What are you going to do?"

"I'm not going to take that job, that's for sure."

Christina looked at me.

"Don't even look at me. You know that this whole situation is obscene. I am *so* not interested any more. I have a beautiful baby to go home to, and he can keep his extended hours and endless travel for someone else."

"What! No, I agree with you. It would be crazy to take it after all of this."

"Oh, okay. You made a face, so I thought that you thought I wasn't making the right decision."

"Nope. You're doing the right thing. Dennis messed up on this one."

Then there was a knock on my door.

"I knew I should've just headed home," I said to Christina. "Come in."

It was Mark and William, colleagues who were also in the meeting.

"That was a short meeting," Christina said.

"Yeah, I think you were the only thing on the agenda," William said.

"I'm not going to take the job, guys," I said.

"She's not going to take the job," Christina added.

"I know that it wasn't presented well," Mark said. "But you can *really* revitalize this thing. We really need you, Bailey. This has impacted all of our departments. You know that we were rooting for you to get the role in the first place."

Aww. "I appreciate that. I went from wanting it so bad to despising it when Stephen got it. Dennis didn't recognize my value. But you know who does?" I asked.

"Who?" William asked reluctantly.

"My baby girl. I'm going home guys," I said. "Thanks but no thanks."

Christina looked at the guys and raised her shoulders.

"Okay. We tried," Mark said.

"Will you think about it?" William asked.

"Don't make me lie to you, William."

He nodded, and they left.

"Do you think Dennis put them up to that?" I asked Christina and crossed my arms.

"Who knows? I don't know who he is anymore. I'm sure Dennis will still try to persuade you."

"I doubt it. Well, he may leave a Post-it note on my monitor or some other indirect, pathetic approach so he doesn't have to face me."

"Yeah. Ugh, what a shame."

"Anyway … any weekend plans?" I asked.

"No. We're going to take it easy. I think one of the girl's friends has a birthday party on Sunday. Gosh, I'm starting to hate those. I just want to be in my PJs all weekend. You know."

"Yeah, I know what you mean. That's my plan for the weekend unless Olivia drags me somewhere to do something. When I was pregnant I couldn't go anywhere during most of my third trimester, and now I'm making it up to her big time."

"Yeah, I bet. I wonder if *Bryce* is free," she said with a mischievous grin.

"Bryce? Why?"

"Hmm? Nothing."

"No, that's something. Wait, did you not come to lunch on purpose to—"

There was another knock on the door.

"Come in," I said. It was Dawn, our director of human resources.

"Hi, ladies. Christina, I was told that you might be in here. Do you have a minute?"

"Sure," Christina replied. Dawn just looked at her, so Christina headed toward the door.

"Hey, if I don't see you enjoy as much of your weekend as possible," I said to Christina.

"Yeah, you too," she said and left with Dawn.

I grabbed my handbag and left before anyone else came in wanting to chat. As I walked down the hall, I peeked into Christina's office. Dawn and one other person from HR were standing near Christina's desk. Dennis and someone else that I couldn't identify were also in the room. Christina looked uncomfortable. I wondered what was going on. I guess I had lingered too long because a couple of them looked up at me, so I walked off. Then I sent Christina a text message telling her to call me as soon as she could.

I couldn't get out of the building quick enough. I thought about Dennis's stunt at the meeting and was angry all over again. I didn't feel like going home just yet. I mean, I couldn't wait to nibble Jade's cheeks, but I felt like having an adult beverage with a friend first—especially since I could finally have an adult beverage after the restrictions were finally lifted. *Who would be available that doesn't have kids to care for? Hmm, that would be … no one. I should call Lisa. Is that the liquor talking? I haven't had a drink yet, though. Hmm … That's either a cool idea or a terrible idea. She loved a good mojito as much as I did, but I probably shouldn't talk to either of my sisters about work-related issues.*

They didn't really identify with corporate America, and, according to what Aunt Janet said that day, I think they took it as me showing off about my "high-level job," as they called it, when I really just wanted to vent and get advice from my big sisters. All these years they'd interpreted the things I'd said as pretentiousness. I mean, in my defense, it had been pretty ridiculous. Once I accidentally left my car in neutral, stepped out of it for something and my car ended up running over my foot—and broke my foot! When I told my sisters— from the hospital, mind you—one sister said, "Oh, was it your *Benz*?" and the other said, "Were you wearing your *Louboutin's* at the time or some sensible flats?" *Because flats are known to sustain moving vehicles? Really, that's what you ask me next? The only red on the bottom of my shoes was blood—dammit! What the hell? I guess I only deserve sympathy if the city bus hits me while I'm wearing shoes from Fayva. Remember Fayva? No? Okay, fine.*

I decided to forgo companionship laced with alcohol, and I just headed home—after a little* shopping *(*a lot)*. As I approached my door, I heard Jade making all types of wonderful sounds on the other side. When she heard my key in the door, she got quiet because she knew it was *me*. She'd stop and look at the door waiting for me to come in.

"Hello, my darling!" I said as I entered, before even knowing where in the apartment Jade was located. My mom was bouncing her on her lap, and Jade's body was totally turned toward the door trying to see if it was *me* coming in. This warmed my heart every time. By now, my shoes were off, my bags were on the foyer table, and I was reaching for Jade, who serenaded me with a melody of assorted sounds and excitement—my favorite soundtrack. *Who needs wine ... that much. I hope there is wine in the house.*

"Jade! Hey, Mom. How was your day?" She couldn't take her eyes off Jade, and she'd been with her all day. *Now that's addiction.*

"It was good."

I extracted Jade from mom's arms. *Seriously, must I go through this every time?* Then with Jade in my arms, I located some wine, which I placed in the refrigerator. Then I took it out and placed it in the freezer. *Why wait thirty minutes for chilled wine when you can wait ten instead?*

"I'm heading home, honey. Remember, your dad and I have that dinner tonight?"

"Oh, yeah. But it's in Manhattan. Why doesn't he just bring your stuff here, so you don't have to trek to Brooklyn to get dressed only to come back to the city?"

"I need to make sure that what your dad is wearing is decent. If I let him get dressed and then head here to get me, it'll be too late for me to fix him."

"Gotcha."

"Okay, I laid out the pajamas Jade should wear tonight and be sure to bathe her before she gets too sleepy. And add a little applesauce to her milk when—"

"Mom?"

"Yeah?"

"Seriously?"

"What?"

"Nothing, Mom. Nothing. Come on Jade." I got up and my mom took Jade right out of my arms.

"Let me just give her a good night kiss before I go. Good night my darling. Aww ..."

I stood there as she showered Jade with kisses and then straightened Jade's top. *Because it'll stay straight now, of course.* When she was done, she handed her back to me and I just looked at her.

"Are you okay?"

I nodded.

"Bye girls." When Mom left, it was like ten people had exited. The energy in the room was then comfortable and light.

"Looks like it's just me and you, Jade. Just you and me, Snikums." *Aw, why do you smell? I may as well give you a warm bath now while I'm de-funking you.* "Okay, Booboo. Let's go and get you all cleaned up."

I played with Jade a good hour after I gave her a warm bath. She was my absolute joy. I wore us both out because she started to doze off. "Not yet, sweetie. Mommy has to feed you." I warmed a bottle for her and was then able to put her to bed with peace of mind.

Wine time!

On Sunday, Bryce stopped by to get my opinion on some shirts that he purchased and he shared an article about the ongoing Klinsar case. He texted me from the department store and wanted my opinion but the pics he sent weren't clear so I told him to just buy them and show me in person.

"This one is simple. White, blue stripe; it works, right?" he asked as he held up a dress shirt.

"Eh," I said.

"Eh?"

"Yeah, Bryce they're all super plain. And they look like shirts that you already have."

"Men don't have all the frilly options that women have."

"Nor should they."

"True. You know what I mean."

"Just because your color and silhouette options aren't as vast as ours—don't be jealous, by the way—it doesn't mean that you have to wear … this. Where'd you get these anyway?"

He looked at his receipt and then he handed it to me.

"I don't even know what this—it's a men's store?" I asked.

"Yeah, and none of this was cheap either."

"That just makes me feel sorrier for you."

"Ha, ha, ha."

"Look, take this stuff back and I'll go with you somewhere better to pick out some sharp pieces."

"Thanks. Alright, I'll go return these now."

"Yeah, hurry before they become a McDonalds. I assure you they won't be in business for long selling menswear."

Bryce shook his head and said, "Do you think we can go this week? I need to update my wardrobe."

"Let's shoot for Saturday."

"Okay."

When Bryce left, Mom came out of the kitchen.

"I think he likes you."

"You think so?"

"Oh yeah, but you can do better."

"You don't like Bryce?"

"Eric was just very handsome and had charisma —"

"Mom. Are you really comparing him to my unfaithful, arrogant, dead husband?"

"I'm just saying. He's no Eric."

"Thank God for that. And let's stick to *not* saying Eric's name as we have been, okay?"

"Sorry."

That really irked me. I didn't know why I even cared what she thought. Listening to her about men in the past is why I married Eric's ass. He wasn't my type but she meddled and insisted that I'd regret not marrying him. I'd felt insecure around him from the first day and ignored my gut all the way to the altar. *Thanks, Mom.*

It was a rainy Monday morning, and the streets were congested. I peered out my taxi window, and no one was moving, but I was in no hurry. The rain had fizzled to a drizzle by the time I got to the office, which was great for my hair. Christina's office was dark. She was usually there before me. She must have been caught in some of the traffic. Or what if she was not here because of whatever went down with her last Friday afternoon? She hadn't called me. I guess I could have called her too, but I totally forgot. *Damn.*

I had a conference call. If she wasn't here by the end of it, I'd call her.

An hour later there was still no Christina, so I called her at home.

"Hey, missy, why aren't you here?"

"Where do I start?"

"Christina, what happened?"

"Remember on Friday when HR came to see me?" *Oh no.*

"Yeah."

"Well, apparently there was an accounting error on an invoice that I signed off on months ago. And it's going to cost the company seven hundred and twenty *thousand* dollars."

"What! How?"

"Melody was off by a decimal point, so she billed the client $80,000 instead of $800,000. I didn't notice it when I signed off on it. And of course the client didn't mention it." Melody was Christina's assistant.

"Oh man …"

"I know."

"I mean, it's a lot of money, but it was an accident. We call the client, we get them to pay the difference—"

"The client isn't in business anymore."

"Oh."

"That's not it. Tyler and I did business with the client's wife a few months ago too. That investment property that we bought was from her, and she sold it to us at a significant discount. We remodeled the place, and she recommended some people, which resulted in some more concessions. They're insinuating that the *accounting error* may have been intentional on my part so that the client's wife could, in turn, grant my husband and me savings on the property."

"No way!"

"Yes, way. And I'm trying to convince them that that wasn't the case. That's not what happened."

"You don't have to convince me. You know I believe you. How'd they even find out about your dealings with his wife?"

"I talked about it here freely at the time. We were excited about the purchase. That's another thing; wouldn't I have hidden that information if I were up to no good? I'm just so mad. They'd think that I would do that? Me?"

"I can't believe this. What happens now?"

"I'm on paid leave for a week pending further investigation."

"Are you kidding me?"

"I wish I was."

"Christina ..."

"I know. It sucks. I don't know what's going to happen."

"Can Dennis do anything? He'd go to bat for you."

"He's trying to see what he can do, but since HR and legal are involved, his hands may be tied. I don't know."

"This is ludicrous. How are you feeling? What are you thinking?"

"I'm kind of numb honestly. I'm not allowed to contact any of my clients, so I have no idea what they've been told. I had to leave my laptop at work when I left on Friday. It all seemed so final."

"Gee whiz. I'll find out what I can. You know I will. They're probably just telling your clients that you're out of the office but I'll find out. Let me send an email to your work address now and see if they've added an 'Out of Office' reply message on your behalf."

"I did that, there isn't one. Not yet anyway."

"Okay, I'll try again later and will let you know if they do. Do you know any employment attorneys?"

"No. Tyler does, but I haven't told him yet."

"Christina! You have to tell your husband."

"I will, but he's out of town on business and is mega-stressed already with his own job. I don't want him worrying about me while he's away; he needs to focus. I'll tell him when he gets back. He knows I'm home, but we didn't get into the *whys*."

"But you can't wait a week to get legal advice."

"I know. I've reached out to Tyler's friend in the meantime."

"Okay, good. Have they been able to offer any guidance?"

"Not yet. The attorney is currently in China on vacay and not answering any email. I think he's back tomorrow, though."

"What about asking Bryce?" I asked.

"I will. I'm hoping this goes away first. If not, I'll call him."

"Okay. Let me think … what else …"

"You're the best, Bailey."

"Please. Let me know if there's anything I can do. Anything. I'll have my ears to the wall here. Whatever I find out, I'll let you know, even if it means that I have to talk to Dennis."

"Okay, thanks."

"Let me bring you lunch later. I want to see you."

"Lunch sounds good."

"Okay, I'll call when I'm on my way."

"Okay."

"See you soon."

"See you."

Damn. Poor Christina. How can they even suspect her of such a thing — she's been kicking ass here for over a decade. They can't let her go for something like this, right? I couldn't even imagine her not being here. Ugh! Now I'm sad …

Carrie was now standing in my doorway with an arm full of folders. *Happy Monday to me.*

She said, "There's a new guy here. I thought he was interviewing, but Dennis has been showing him around, and then he took him to Stephen's old office."

"Really? What the—" I stood in my doorway and Dennis was talking with some guy in front of Stephen's former office. Then I realized that I didn't care, so I walked back into my office.

"Is he replacing Stephen?"

"I have no idea. But I'm sure we'll all know before the day is out. So whatcha got for me?" I asked, referring to the stack of folders in her tiny arms.

"Oh, these I just need to file in your office. But these two need your signature." She handed me two invoices. Before signing, I checked the numbers and data … twice.

Lunch at Christina's was so much fun. We're silly under any circumstance; you would never have known that we had a job crisis on our hands. I was glad that I stopped by, and she was too. I told her about the visitor and potential replacement for Stephen. She thought she knew the guy. Since I didn't know his name or anything, all I could do was describe him to her. She thought he interviewed for another role some time last year; that position ended up being put on hold by the department. That would make some sense, then, opposed to bringing him in in what seemed to be out of the blue.

Speaking of the devil, Mr. Newguy was walking across the street heading toward me.

"Hey, Bailey. I wasn't formally introduced to you this morning."

"Hello," I said.

He shook my hand. "I'm Chase. Dennis has told me a lot about you."

"Welcome, Chase. Are you the new senior manager?" Chase was cute. And he had a trusting face too. But he was too tall for my taste. *I know, when does a woman ever say that a guy is too tall?* I was five-seven, and my comfort zone was five-eleven to six-two when it came to guys; otherwise, it just got too ridiculous. *I can't hear him; he can't see me — who has time?* Chase looked like he was about six-five or something crazy like that.

"Yes, I am. Dennis mentioned that he offered the role to you, but you turned it down?" I heard the question mark at the end of his sentence but chose to ignore it.

"Where are you joining us from, Chase?" I asked. By now, we were walking back to the building together.

"I was with Colby Phillips on the West Coast."

"Oh, okay. So you have direct experience with the West Coast market. That's really good."

"Yeah, it should come in handy."

"It'll definitely come in handy. So when were you contacted about this position with us?" I had to know.

"Honestly, Dennis called me yesterday when I was out playing golf. We talked for almost two hours. When I came in this morning, it was mostly to continue our conversation but I was sold. We sealed the deal an hour ago."

Interesting. I couldn't be mad at that. Dennis knew that I wasn't going to accept the position and the show must go on. Unless he plotted this from the very beginning "offer" me the job in front of everyone as an obvious runner-up so I'd turn it down and then he'd get another *male* in there. You know what? I didn't even care anymore. I hoped Chase would do a kickass job.

"Well, welcome aboard, Chase. Let me know if I can be of any assistance." By now, we were in the building lobby.

"Actually, I could use your help, if you don't mind. At first glance, I couldn't make out some of the data that um ... Stephen left behind. Could I pick your brain on a few things?"

"Sure, I don't mind. Set up some time on my calendar. I'd be happy to help."

"I really appreciate it."

"No problem."

I sent Christina a text message to let her know that Chase was the guy's name, and he was indeed the new senior manager. She confirmed that he was the person she was thinking of and said he was really cool. I told her that I chatted with him for a bit, and he did seem cool. She asked if he was still cute. I replied, "Yeah, he is, for a tall guy." She texted me back "He's no Bryce though" with a smiley face. I didn't reply. *Cupid.*

Bryce had actually texted me and asked if this Friday evening would work to go shopping and maybe grab a bite. I hadn't responded to him yet.

Christina came by with her girls on Sunday, and we hung in the kitchen while the girls helped Mom with Jade. Human resources had asked Christina to be out an additional week pending further investigation of her case.

"I know that you were already going crazy sitting at home for the first week. Now you have to do it again. I'm sorry you're going through this."

"Thanks. It suuucks!"

"I know. What are you thinking?"

"I'm waiting to see what the outcome is at the end of my leave, which I thought was going to be last Friday."

"Have you told Tyler yet?"

"Yeah, I told him."

"What does he recommend?"

"Oh, you mean have I told him the truth? No, I haven't told him that."

"Christina!"

"He has a major job crisis of his own. I can't tell him everything right now."

"Is he in jeopardy of losing his job?"

"No, nothing like that, but they are stressing him out to the point where he's thinking of quitting. I can't tell if he's all talk or if he's actually sprucing up his résumé."

"You might want to find out before he comes home with some news of his own."

"You're right. That's true ... why aren't we drinking wine yet?"

"Where are my manners?" I said and grabbed a bottle of chilled wine and two wine goblets.

"I *love* coming here. You always have the wines I can't afford."

"So, you visit me because of my wine selection?"

"Nooo, it's not the reason … just the incentive."

"Oh that's much better," I said. "Thanks for those baby food recipes. Jade loves them."

"You're welcome. I used to make them for my girls all the time. But I loved the ones that you came up with too. You pureed the vegetables and fruit together?"

"Yeah, but only certain combinations work if you're going to store any in the fridge. Some turn color the next day even if they're still fresh. But of course, mentally I can't stand that it turns brown, so I'd throw it away."

"Yeah, I would too."

"What made you think of doing it?"

"The preservatives in the supermarket baby food. I only cook healthy food for myself, so I have to feed my baby healthy food, though I enjoy decadent treats occasionally when I dine out."

"All in moderation."

"Exactly."

"Is that how you got your body to snap back so fast after having Jade?"

"No, that was good ol' stress. And it wasn't with *three-tier interlocking reinforcement supercalifragilistic* sneakers like you."

"Ha, ha! Hey, whatever works, right?"

"Um hmm, says the woman with zero-percent body fat."

"Well, everyone can't be me."

Christina handed me my cell phone that was vibrating next to her. I looked at it and pressed "Ignore."

"Why didn't you answer it?" she asked. She saw that it was Bryce calling.

"I can call him back later."

"But will you?"

"What do you mean?"

"He asked about you. Said he's left you a few messages but hasn't heard from you."

"I'm going to call him."

"Hmm."

"What hmm?"

"Nothing. He's a good guy, that's all."

"Yeah, Bryce is great I just—"

"Ugh, Bryce," said Mom who walked into the kitchen.

"Ahh, now it makes sense," said Christina.

"What?" I asked. "It's not because my mom—"

"Um, hmm," Christina said then asked my mom, "Are the girls helping you with Jade or are they in nuisance-mode now?"

"Those girls are just darling. They've been wonderful," Mom replied.

"Oh good. May I hold Jade before we go? I promise I'll give her back. I'll try to anyway." Christina was fully aware of my mother's Jade-obsession, so she knew she couldn't just go and pick her up as one would in a normal environment.

"Sure. Come on," Mom replied and led the way into the living room. Christina and I looked at each other with surprise and followed behind her.

Jade was in her playpen, and Christina's girls were singing and dancing for her. *Jade loved it! She had the most adorable laugh.* Christina picked her up out of the playpen, and

Jade agreed willingly. I took photos of them with my phone—as if I didn't have several of them together already.

"I think she actually knows me now," Christina said.

"Of course she does. Are you kidding me? Outside of Olivia, my parents and Edna-the-nanny, you guys are the only other ones that she sees regularly. She knows her Aunt Christina." Christina loved hearing that. It was true, though. If someone came over that Jade didn't recognize, she ignored them. *And they shouldn't even think of trying to touch her.*

"Do you call your nanny *Edna-the-nanny* to everyone?"

"Actually, we do," Mom chimed in. "I have a good friend named Edna, so we specify with Edna-the-nanny."

"Ahh," Christina replied. She didn't care. Mom lost her at "actually."

"Edna-the-nanny can't stand Mom," I whispered to Christina.

"Really? Why?"

I tilted my head. Christina knew that my mom had her ways.

"Nothing Edna does is right or mom's way," I continued to whisper. "I'm waiting for the day that Edna throws a pot at her. Funny thing is it made me feel better that it wasn't just me that she did it to. She made me feel incompetent and insecure as a new mother the first couple of months. Anyway …"

"Wow. How long before Edna-the-nanny lets your mom have it?"

I shrugged.

"Okay, girls. Let's get ready to go," Christina said.

"*Noo,*" the girls replied.

"Okay, I'll just have to get ice cream for myself then," she sang in pure manipulation. Her girls hopped up, put Jade's toys in her playpen, and grabbed their shoes. *The power of carbs starts young.*

After they left and Mom was putting Jade down for a nap, I sat on the sofa and stared at my cell phone. *Why was I ignoring Bryce? Was I allowing Mom's opinion to carry that much weight?* I should've just called him right then. But I didn't.

COIN INCREASE

Another workweek without Christina just wasn't the same. This week dragged out for sure, but thank God it was *Friday Eve*—only one more day to go, and then it's the weekend. Plus Christina told me she'd be back at work on Monday. I was not sure if everything was cleared with HR, but it sounded like a step in the right direction at least.

I'd been working with Chase, getting him acclimated on how we did things at knirD, and he was really cool; an extremely smart guy with a great sense of humor—this company didn't deserve him.

It was lunchtime, so I decided to pick up some sushi. While I waited on my order, I saw Bryce across the street, then I turned around so that he wouldn't see me. It had been a few weeks and I still hadn't returned any of his calls. After a minute a so, I peeked to see if he was still in the vicinity. He was and he was with a woman, a pretty woman. *Hmm.*

"Dynamite roll special!"

"Oh, sorry. That's mine. Thank you," I said. *I wonder how many times he said that before I actually heard him.*

I texted Christina: "I just saw Bryce out with an attractive woman."

Christina replied: "Why do you care?"

She had a point. Why did I care?

When I got back to work, Carrie greeted me with messages and requests.

"Two messages," said Carrie. "And I need next Tuesday off. One message from Curtis, he needs the mock ups. The other message is from Doug Stanford at Klinsar."

"Klinsar?"

"Yes. What's wrong?" My expression must have startled her.

"Nothing. What did he say?"

"He asked if I had another number for you because he'd been trying you on your mobile phone."

I checked my phone and it needed to be charged. *Of course.*

"Thanks Carrie." I took the messages from her and then entered my office. I was no longer hungry. Seeing Bryce and then getting a call from Klinsar left me feeling uneasy. I stared at my desk phone and watched the time on it change until eight minutes had passed. Then it rang and scared the hell out of me.

"Bailey Bryant ... Sure ... Okay, bye." It was just an update from the QA team.

I knew that I wouldn't have been able to get any work done unless I called Klinsar and / or Bryce. I bit the bullet.

"Doug Stanford."

Cleared my throat. "Yes, this is Bailey Bryant. I have a message from you."

"Mrs. Bryant. Yes, thank you so much for returning my call. Can I put you on hold for one moment?"

"Sure."

I held on the line listening to eighties music and wondered why Doug had called me. What did anyone from Klinsar have to say to me at this point? These people made me nervous, and I was certain that they knew more about Eric's final days than they led the media or police or me to believe.

"Mrs. Bryant?" I was on speakerphone now.

"Yes, I'm here."

"Thank you so much for holding. I've been joined by Cliff Myers and Nick Parker who—"

"Yes, I know Cliff and Nick." They were the top, big-wig executives at Klinsar on the legal and finance side.

"Mrs. Bryant, is there any way that you could join us for dinner this evening or lunch tomorrow? We'll be in Manhattan."

I didn't know how to respond. I didn't want to sit and eat with them but I wanted to know what this was all about.

"May I ask, what's the purpose of this meeting?" *Silence.*

"It would be better if we spoke in person, Mrs. Bryant."

I didn't respond immediately. I wanted to know what this was about but needed to get to Bryce first and get his take on what I should do.

"Lunch tomorrow would be better."

"Great, can we give you the details in the morning?"

"Sure."

When I hung up, I immediately called Bryce and got his voice mail—quick. *Did he just reject my call?* I left him a message but didn't mention Klinsar. I thought my mind was going to be clear after I made the calls but things were even more ambiguous now.

The next morning, I put on my sharpest suit and looked like I owned Manhattan. I didn't want to look as uncomfortable as I felt when I met with the Klinsar folks for lunch. If they had planned to intimidate me in any way, I wanted to give the impression that *I was not having it.* Dennis probably thought that I was interviewing elsewhere because even I didn't get this snazzy on Friday's.

Bryce hadn't called me back the night before, which was odd, and I'd called him twice. I thought about him and that woman and assumed that they had probably spent the evening together, giving him no time to call me back. I shouldn't have cared but I did. I really wanted to talk to him about the call from Klinsar, get his thoughts, and ask him to go to the lunch with me—if I should have gone at all. *I should've called him weeks ago.*

"You look very nice, Bailey," said Edna-the-nanny.

"Oh, thank you Edna."

"You always look nice but today you look ... official, like you mean business."

"I do. It's the look I was going for, thanks," I said. "My mom will be here a bit later today. She has an appointment so she won't get here until three o'clock."

"Good. I hope her appointment runs late." *Damn. Tell me how you really feel.*

"I know that my mom can be a challenge, Edna. I'm sorry. I guess she's just being a grandmother."

"I've worked with many grandmothers. Your mom is … have a good day, Bailey." Then she walked away. I guess she'd felt that was better than whatever was going to come out of her mouth. I had to have a talk with Mom. It was one thing to drive me crazy but I needed Edna. And I needed Edna to be happy.

I called Bryce again an hour before my lunch meeting with Klinsar and again, no callback from him. I decided to intentionally go to the meeting ten minutes late so that all three of the guys from Klinsar would be there. The last thing I wanted was to have to endure small-talk waiting for any of them to arrive.

When I got there, the host escorted me to the table and I saw that all three of the men were there. My walk to the table was straight out of the movies—I had a powerful stride, in what felt like slow motion, a large clutch under my arm, and oversized sunglasses, which concealed the fear in my eyes. Before I got to the table, they all stood, hands extended once I got there. They all greeted me by name but I didn't say a word. I took off my sunglasses, put my clutch on the table, and then shook each hand.

Then I said, "Gentlemen," before I took my seat.

They all sat and I felt each butterfly leave my stomach one by one. *I can do this.*

"Mrs. Bryant, thanks so much for meeting us on such short notice," said Doug.

I nodded.

"We know that you're busy, Mrs. Bryant, so we'll get right to why we asked you here today," said Nick. "We can't begin to imagine what you've been going through. Losing Eric has had many implications, we know."

I didn't respond. I had no idea what he was getting at. *I wish Bryce was here.*

"There's no way to estimate or recompense the current and future scarcities that Eric's absence will cause, but we'd like to—in our most sincerest attempt, Mrs. Bryant – offset some of your current and future obligations, especially with a new child," said Nick.

I shifted in my seat when they mentioned my child. Ironically, my shift made them shift. *Were they nervous?* I felt a little more powerful in that moment.

"Nick," I said and looked at my watch. "Can you tell me what you're getting at?"

Doug jumped in and said, "Mrs. Bryant, we would like to give you … something." Then he pulled a folder out of his briefcase and handed me some papers.

I read through the first page and noticed that they were also trying to read me. I kept a poker face the entire time, even when I got to the next-to-last paragraph and saw an amount listed that had six zero's—pre-decimal. *They want to pay me off.* I went back to the first page and skimmed through it again. By now, two of the men were drinking water, still with their eyes on me. "Will not pursue us for *future damages* …", "Will not disclose the details of this agreement or its terms …" —I was rereading all the "will not's" and "do not's" in the agreement.

"So," I finally uttered. "This is a settlement and non-disclosure agreement?"

"Not a settlement, per se. We aren't disputing parties and Eric was definitely a loss to us as well—"

"What Clint means is, we acknowledge that many deficits have been caused by the loss of your husband, one of them likely being financial," said Nick. "And because Eric was so highly esteemed, loved, and the reason behind much of the success at Klinsar, we genuinely feel compelled to offset some of that for you, if you'll allow us, Mrs. Bryant."

"I see," I said. "I'll need to review this with my attorney and consider it further, of course."

"Yes, of course," said Doug.

I put the agreement in my clutch and stood. They all followed suit.

"Gentlemen," I said.

"Thanks again for meeting with us, Mrs. Bryant. And you have my number, please call me with any questions you may have," said Doug.

"Thank you, Doug."

When I got outside, I felt like someone should have yelled "Cut!" because that was straight out of a movie. *Did they really just offer me millions of dollars?* When I got in the taxi, I reread the agreement again and stared at the proposed figure. *Is this in US dollars?* I searched for stipulations, inconspicuous verbiage, and good ol' fine print. I checked my phone to see if Bryce had called while I had it on silent. *No call.* Okay, now I'm mad. What the hell? I wanted to call him and tell him about this huge update, get him to review the contract and give me legal counsel—especially since he was initially so involved in the Klinsar case with me. But I decided against it. The agreement was only two pages long. When I got back to the office, I planned to Google each sentence myself and make sure that the agreement said what I thought it said.

I did it. I dissected the Klinsar agreement. They basically wanted me to agree to not sue them at any time in the future, under any circumstances and to not let it be known to anyone that they were basically paying me off. This likely because they'd plan to go after Bryner and get a ridiculous amount of money from them, which they wanted me to have no part of. I was actually okay with that. If I signed this agreement, Jade and I would be set. If I signed this agreement, Klinsar and I would be done, and I'd never have to feel uneasy by the mention of their name. Klinsar and I would be *cool*. I'd wondered before if they had anything to do with Eric's disappearance and then ... exit. But I stopped thinking that was a possibility by the time we had the funeral.

I looked at the highlighted pages and Post-it notes all over my desk from the agreement research I'd just conducted and, like clockwork, I got a call.

"Bailey, you have a call on line one from Doug with Klinsar," said Carrie.

"This is Bailey."

"Mrs. Bryant, this is Doug. I'm sorry to bother you."

"No bother."

"I wanted to get your initial thoughts about the agreement, the financial piece, any questions."

Hmm … why's he so anxious.

"I've reviewed it, and I don't have any questions."

"I see." He was thinking. "If you did intend to sign the agreement, is there anything that could influence you to sign it sooner than later?"

Someone was pressuring him to get me to sign this.

"Such as?" I asked.

"We could increase the remuneration." *More millions?*

"I see. When you say increase—"

"If you sign today, we can double the amount."

I coughed.

"I could be convinced to sign it today at that amount."

"Mrs. Bryant, I can email you an updated pdf of the agreement reflecting the new amount in the next fifteen minutes and have the funds transferred to your bank by close of business today." *Say what?*

"Can you email me a revised page two only? I don't want to have to reread it all again."

"I can definitely do that Mrs. Bryant."

"I'll await your email then Doug."

My armpits were wet. I still couldn't believe that any of this had really transpired. OMG! And I couldn't tell anyone about it. I was rocking in my seat. Five minutes later "You've got mail!" *Well, you know what I mean.* When I woke up that morning, I had no idea that my life was going to be impacted so much.

I opened Doug's email attachment and saw that the figure had been changed. *Wow.* I compared all of the verbiage to the original agreement and nothing had been changed. I emailed Doug and he was on his way to my office.

I walked home from work that night. I was in a daze. This was confirmed by the fact that I didn't stop in any stores along the thirty-block journey. I still didn't believe it. "When I get the funds I'll believe it," I told myself.

As I approached my apartment door, I heard a loud exchange coming from inside. *Oh damn.*

"Your way isn't the only way that works," said Edna to my mom.

"Jade is my granddaughter, not yours," said Mom.

"What is going on?" I asked.

Mom was way too close to Edna's face.

"Bailey, your mother is unreasonable."

"Unreasonable?"

"Yes! Jade is clean and fed and clothed. The fact that it wasn't the bottle you prepared, the suds you drew, or the pajamas you selected—is the issue here. Your issue!" said Edna.

"Look, maybe we—" I attempted.

"My issue?" yelled Mom. "May I remind you that I've raised six children and ten grandchildren, not including Jade."

"You remind me every single day!" said Edna.

Then we heard cries from Jade's room.

"I'll go and—"

"No, Mom. I'll get her."

I sat with Jade in the rocking chair, and she was back to sleep within a few minutes.

"I'll see you on Monday, Bailey," said Edna.

"Not tomorrow?" I asked.

"Not tomorrow." Edna was pissed. I was going to have to fix this quickly. It had definitely gotten out of hand.

When I walked back into the living room, Mom was watching television as if nothing had happened. I grabbed the remote and turned it off.

"Mom, what are you doing?"

"I was trying to watch some television."

"I'm talking about with Edna, Mom. You can't treat her like she's some inexperienced babysitter who doesn't know what she's doing. She's great with Jade and you've been so condescending and rude to her."

"How dare you! You don't even know what happened, and you're taking her side?"

"You need to lower your voice before you wake Jade again. I know exactly what's been going on, Mother. You were treating me the same way. Edna has been a nanny for decades and came with impeccable references—not to mention the children of her own that she's raised. And just because I'm a first-time mom doesn't mean I'm an idiot. God gave me the same maternal instincts that he gave you. You were a first time mother too at one point."

"And I appreciated all of the assistance and wisdom that my mother gave me at the time."

"I'm sure grandma was bearable though." *That did it.*

"I see."

Mom left and I didn't try to stop her. I slumped on the sofa and let my head fall back. Then my cell phone beeped. *Bryce?* No. It was a text alert from my bank. I clicked on it and saw that there was a deposit made to my account. A huge freakin' deposit. *It really happened.* I knew I said that I'd believe it when I got the funds, but I still didn't believe it. "Okay, I'll believe it if the funds are still there come Monday." Then it officially wouldn't be a dream.

MONDAY, THE REMIX

I walked with a different pep in my step Monday morning. Edna showed up early, which I was so thankful for. After Friday, I didn't know if I'd ever see her again. And Christina was going to be back in the office, so things would be back to normal. The sun was shining—well, not really, but I didn't mind as much.

"Hi, Chase."

"Hey, morning, Bailey. How was the weekend?"

"Fantastic. How was yours?"

"Too short."

"I'll give you that."

"Christina's here." He pointed to the break room. He hadn't been here long, but he already knew she was my partner in crime.

"Yay!" I joined Christina who was pouring some coffee.

"Good Monday morning," she said.

"Hey." We walked toward her office. "How's it been so far? Has anyone said anything to you?" I asked.

"Nothing yet, but I'm meeting with Dennis and a few others soon." She sounded nervous. We entered her office, and she closed the door.

"Did you get your laptop back yet?"

"Not yet. I don't know, Bailey ... I thought I was going to be back today to work. A meeting or something, yeah, but now I feel like there's more going on, and I was called in for something that I'm not prepared for."

"Something like what?" She just looked at me. *Did she think that she was getting fired? Oh no.*

"I'll keep you posted."

"Okay. I'll check on you later."

I wanted to ask her if her husband knew the full story yet and what was going on with his own job, but she looked too stressed for me to bring any of that up. Now she had me wonder what was going to happen today.

Three meetings and three cups of coffee later, it was now lunchtime, but I was not hungry. *Caffeine will do that to you.* I needed to find Christina to see what was going on. As soon as I stood up, Christina appeared in my doorway holding a coffee mug.

"I was just coming to find you. I had a tournament of meetings," I said.

"That's Monday's for you."

"Come in, come in. Close the door. So what's going on? Any updates?" I asked.

Christina shrugged, smiled and said, "Nothing really."

"You're smiling now?"

"What else can I do?"

"That's not coffee in your cup, is it?"

"Ha ha," she said and looked inside her cup.

"You had to check?"

"Ha, ha. No, it was coffee. I can't control what's going to happen so why stress over it, you know? Whatever happens, happens."

"Aww, how defeatist of you."

"Defeatist? What the hell would you do?"

"That's the fire I'm looking for! Actually, I may have an idea."

"I'm open to anything."

"Let's see how this thing plays out. I mean has anyone said anything to you at all?"

"Dennis mentioned that the executive team would be meeting this week to discuss it."

"Definitely or maybe? Last week he said that they might meet."

"Now it's definitely, either Thursday or Friday. Dennis said that he'd prep me in case I needed to appear before them."

"Is this like they're going to make a decision on your fate here or get your side of what happened?"

"I think it's the former."

"Christina."

"I know. I got my laptop back, though. But I'm not allowed to contact any clients just yet. I was on LinkedIn this past weekend. I updated my profile and did a preliminary search to see what was out there."

"Let's not go down that road just yet."

"I have to be realistic and proactive."

"I know but let's just see what happens." I knew that that was much easier said than done. Christina waiting for someone else to determine her tomorrow without doing something about it wasn't going to happen.

My cell phone rang, and it was Bryce. *Now he calls me.* As soon as Christina heard the ring, she stood up to give me privacy.

"No, wait. It's just Bryce. Sit."

"It's okay. I need some more coffee anyway," she said and left.

"Hello," I answered.

"Hello." *Okay ...*

"Bryce?"

"Yes. You called me?" I looked at my phone. I didn't like his tone at all.

"I did call you."

"Okay." *Silence.*

"You know what, never mind," I said.

"Okay."

I hung up. What the hell is his problem? Okay, I was wrong to not return his calls for a few weeks. I get it. But he took his time to call me back too. And with an attitude — why call at all. *Ugh.*

I stood to go catch up with Christina but decided to check my bank account online first. *The funds were still in there.* Okay, I officially believed that it wasn't a dream. It happened. I decided to transfer the money to another account at another bank — one that Klinsar didn't have knowledge of, just to be on the safe side.

I went to find Christina and saw that she was in her office with Dennis. Dennis walked out when I walked in. We exchanged a nod. I figured that if he was actually trying to help Christina, I could be polite.

"What was he saying?" I asked.

"He said that I might want to think of resigning before the executive team makes a decision. It would be better for me professionally."

"What! Resign?"

"Right."

"Is that where we are now?"

"Apparently so."

"Would you still get a severance though if you resigned versus being … terminated?"

"Dennis said that he'd make sure that I did."

I twisted my face and said, "Get *that* in writing."

"Yeah …" She looked dejected.

"Wait, I almost forgot why I came in here. Grab your bag. Let's go!" I said excitedly.

"Where are we going?" She had begun to smile. *I have that effect on people.*

"Today is a great day, Christina. Let's go eat. I have ideas."

"Ideas now, plural? Let's do it."

Christina and I headed to Bergdorf's restaurant for lunch, and I could hardly wait to share my new ideas, given the day she'd had and the dismal outlook of her future at knirD.

"So whatcha got? By the way, things with Tyler's job are fine. He made some demands, and his boss came through."

"That's great! I'm so glad to hear that."

"So am I. I told Tyler about what was going on here, and it made my timid, amenable husband take the lead and make things happen. I was so proud and impressed, and turned on. We had a *great* weekend." She raised her eyebrows.

"You dirty girl." We laughed.

"So tell me, tell me. What are these ideas that you have?"

"Well, I recently came into some money—"

"Eric's uh—"

"Yeah, related to that. Well, I was thinking about using some of that money to start a business *with you*."

"With me? What kind of business?"

"Guess. If you guess right, you can be president."

"And if I guess wrong?"

"Customer service rep." We laughed again.

"Well, knowing you, I'm thinking it has something to do with shoes, which I wouldn't be good for. But knowing *us*, the first thing that comes to mind is something food related. More specifically something healthy—for kids?"

I extended my hand and said, "Correct, Madam President."

Christina shook my hand and said, "I am so in."

"Yeah?"

"Absolutely! How long have you been thinking of this?"

"I kinda started thinking about doing something different when I didn't get the senior manager job. But this particular idea was birthed this weekend. It was just me and Jade, no Edna or Mom. I prepared all her meals myself from scratch and she just loved them. But you and I discuss healthy recipe ideas for our girls all the time."

"Yeah, we do. It's actually a great idea for us."

"Isn't it? And now with things the way they are at work, and my coming into come cash, the timing seems perfect."

"It really does. So, what have you come up with so far?" By now, our waitress had come over, but neither of us had reviewed the menu. We listened to the specials of the day; ordered two of those and cocktails.

"I thought of having a chic high-end line of products. We *are* in Manhattan."

"True."

"But also the healthy line, which would be the cash cow. One of the ideas is a two-pack cookie or some snack; one side of the package is light blue, the other side yellow, for instance. One cookie would be for baby, the other for Mom — or Dad. One thing we both discussed and experienced with our girls was convincing them to eat new things, but they always wanted to eat whatever we were eating. So if Mom is eating from the packet, baby will want some too."

"Nice."

"And maybe Mom's is a low-calorie weight-loss version of baby's healthy snack."

"I'm so impressed already."

"Thanks! Also, I thought about …" We sat there for two more hours brainstorming and sharing more ideas than we had enough paper to jot down.

"Okay, so who else are we bringing with us?" Christina asked.

"We think alike! I definitely want to bring Carrie. She's an awesome assistant, but she also has this great knack for social media and can serve us well there. She'd love the opportunity to do more things, and I think she'd want to follow me once I left anyway."

"True and true."

"Given the cause of your current situation, I'm assuming that you won't want to bring your assistant along."

"Not at all. In fact, we need to share and wear many hats initially, so Carrie can be the social media/administrative manager to us both."

"Agreed."

"Who else?"

"Funny thing. I think we should ask Chase."

"Me too!"

"Right? He's so smart, and in the short time at knirD he's made some real progress."

"Do you think we can get him, though? I mean, he's highly compensated, just relocated, and he likes his current job to my knowledge."

"This is true. I honestly don't think we can get him, but we should probably try. The icing on the cake is that it'll piss Dennis off."

"Ha ha. It *so* would."

"Chase hates the constant travel, so that may help us. Plus, he's managing our existing brands and only one new product. When he learns that there's no plan to add to the line, he may lose interest."

"Good point. What about that guy on William's team? The one who had a few ideas about snack items but kept getting shot down? He could be a major asset for us."

"Yeah. Good thinking." I added that to the list.

"Okay, so I need to negotiate a strong severance package and go ahead and plan my exit."

"Yeah. How are you feeling?"

"I'm stoked. Oh my gosh, I can't wait to tell Tyler! I'm going to be up all night thinking of more ideas."

"I'm so excited! And I'm so happy that we're doing this together. I don't know what I would've done if you said you weren't interested. I didn't even think of that option actually. That would've sucked."

"No way. I'm totally in, and the timing couldn't be more perfect."

"Ooh! I know of a great potential office space."

"Yeah, where?"

"It's lower Manhattan, and there's a building south of the pier—"

"Not on that deserted creepy street that you love? The black brick building?"

"Yeah! It's perfect."

"That building is decrepit and so isolated from everything, and there are tons of exterior wires and cables. It can't be healthy for the people inside of it. I'm sure none of them pee straight or have needed a baby shower in decades."

"Christina!" *Funny but so true.* "Okay, how about the one behind it. It's even more affordable."

"Bailey. That whole block, it's … it's not a place you go, it's a place you end up."

"Fine," I said, and chuckled. "I'll keep looking. Oh, let me take a picture of us at our *first planning meeting,*" I said and grabbed my phone.

"Oh, gosh."

The next couple of weeks were extremely busy. Christina departed knirD—*with a bang*! The executive team publicly awarded her for her service and overall; it was a nice, grand exit. Dennis came through, and she received a generous severance package as well. The best part was that Christina left the company happy, and it showed.

We decided that I was going to stay on board for a little while to find talent to bring with us. We already had a few employees that we planned to poach, but given the nature of knirD's parallel business, we figured there might be people to bring with us, now or in the future, whom we hadn't thought of. So, I went through organizational charts, performance reviews, and good old office gossip to find the best of the best.

I approached Carrie about our plans and made her an offer that she accepted before even hearing all the specifics. She was excited to say the least. She stayed at knirD with me and helped with some data gathering, which proved invaluable. Christina and I met for lunch every day at her place to build the company, layer by layer. We were able to secure office space but wouldn't be able to occupy it for a month. That ended up being the perfect target date for us to get a few things completed by.

Back at home, things were progressive. Jade was my taste-tester. Mom and I had made up but she was being passive-aggressive. She called often but stopped coming by to help me with Jade. Edna just increased her hours, which was a peaceful solution for us all. Mom wanted to *show me* how much I needed her. *So, Edna then showed me how much we didn't.*

I hadn't spoken to Bryce since the annoying, brief conversation that we had. I tried not to think about it but when I did, it made me sad. And this particular Friday evening … I was thinking about it.

Edna had put Jade to sleep and was about to head home for the evening. I was on the sofa, staring at the television that was off.

"You okay?" Edna asked, as she put her jacket on.

"I'm fine. Just tired, I guess."

"Well, that little girl won't be up before the morning. So feel free to relax."

"Thanks Edna. Enjoy your weekend."

As soon as she left, my phone beeped. *It was Bryce.* He'd sent me a text message that said, "Hi."

I replied: "Hi there." Then I deleted "there" and pressed Send.

He replied: "Could we talk?"

I replied: "Sure." *My phone rang.*

"I don't like that we're not speaking," he said.

"I don't either, Bryce."

"What happened?"

"I don't know …" *I knew.* I let my mom get in my head, and I was stupid, basically.

"Me neither. So what now?"

"We could just pick up where we left off."

"Okay," he said. "Do you have plans for the weekend?"

"Chillin' with Jade all weekend long."

"Cool. Mind if I stop by tomorrow?"

"Tomorrow's good."

"Evening?"

"See you then." I hung up and smiled.

The next day Jade reminded me why a nanny—and grandmother, to be honest – were essential for not only her well-being but mine too. She was fussy and teething. She didn't take an afternoon nap and I paid for it dearly. By the time I'd finally been able to put her down to bed, it was six o'clock and I was beat. Next thing I knew, Bryce texted me and was on his way over.

I had milk stains and a couple of other unidentifiable smudges on my clothes, so I had to change. I washed my face, put on some leggings, a t-shirt and some socks, and then I got cozy on the sofa when I realized I was hungry. *Maybe I should ask Bryce to pick something up.* I went into the kitchen and grabbed some hummus and pita chips. *This will do.* I flipped through some channels then checked my DVR list. *The Voice.* Perfect. I loved *The Voice.* This was turning out to be a good Saturday. *I'm getting old.* I got comfortable and turned the volume up. *Adam is such a cutie. Let me just pause it on him for a few minutes ...*

Jack called to tell me Bryce was here; I walked to the foyer and fixed my hair and checked out my face in the mirror. *Why am I checking out my face in the mirror?* I let Bryce in and we shared a long hug. *It had been too long.*

"Thanks for not ringing the doorbell. Jade is sleeping."

"I figured I should take the precaution."

"Nice *man-bag.*"

"It's a briefcase. It just has a long strap." He handed me his jacket. I pointed to the coat rack right next to him. "You're quite the hostess, you know."

"Aw, thank you."

"Do you have anything to eat? I'm starving?"

"Aw, man. I almost called you to pick something up. Should we order food?"

"I'm in the mood for pizza actually."

"When aren't you in the mood for pizza?"

"When I'm in the mood for Mexican food."

"True. Let's order pizza then. What crap do you want on your half?"

He chuckled and said, "Why do my toppings have to be crap?"

"Because it clogs your arteries, veins, capillaries, and ability to have a lot of birthdays."

"But I work out. Feel this," he said and pointed to his stomach. I reached for his stomach then he grabbed my hand. "I didn't think you were really going to feel it. I haven't been to the gym in a couple of weeks. Feel this instead," he said and flexed his bicep.

I touched his bicep and said, "You're 0 for 2, Bryce. Let's just order pizza."

"Ouch!"

"I'm just kidding. That's the most impressive bicep that I've felt all day. Pizza toppings?"

"Ouch again. I guess I'll have spinach, tomatoes, and mushrooms."

"Perfect! I'm so proud of you. That's what I was going to get. Are you sure you don't want any swine on your half?"

"No, I'm not sure, but I've been judged enough tonight."

"This is true."

I called in the pizza order while battling Bryce for the remote control. He acted as if he didn't love *The Voice* as much as I did, but then he always got wrapped up in whom the coaches selected.

When the pizza came, we talked and got caught up on each other's lives. I didn't tell him about the meeting with and money from Klinsar. I was tempted to but remembered all the "shall not's" and "better don'ts" in the contract. Plus I wasn't yet comfortable with anyone knowing how much money I'd come into. I did tell him about the business plans with Christina. He was very encouraging and supportive. After the chit chat, we both felt like watching a movie. We did, and I had to poke Bryce a few times to keep his noise down, so he wouldn't wake up Jade.

After the movie, and my third yawn, Bryce decided it was time for him to head home. I walked him to the door.

"Thanks for coming by, Bryce."

"Thank you. I had a great time."

I reached for the doorknob and Bryce kissed me—on the lips. *What is he doing?* I looked at him, and then I kissed him on the lips. *What am I doing?* And then we were both just kissing … on the lips … for a while. He held me close, and it was *really* nice. But I still didn't know what I was doing. But I was definitely enjoying it. Then his crotch started moving, and I backed away a little. And we just looked at each other. *Come on, Bryce. Say something.*

"Um, I better get going."

"Okay. Good night."

"Good night," he said and walked out the door. Then he turned back and gave me another nice kiss, and then he left. I closed the door and leaned against it.

Then I cleaned up the living room and drank the remaining wine in Bryce's glass. I drank it more so because Bryce drank from the glass than because of the wine in it. *Why do girls do that?*

I turned the lights out and walked to my bedroom, smiling.

I guess Christina was right.

The next morning, Bryce called me — very early.

"Did I wake you?" he asked.

"Wake me? The only people up this early on a Sunday are pastors and people coming in from the club. Is everything okay?"

"I couldn't sleep," he said. "Look, Bailey ... I don't want to be friends."

I sat up in the bed.

"What?"

"I knew it a few months ago, I felt it even more during our communication hiatus and when I saw you yesterday, it was confirmed," he said. "I want to be more than friends."

"Oh." *Ohhh ...*

"I'm not asking you to respond or anything right now. You're half awake and might not even know who you're talking to right now," he said. I chuckled. "But I needed to let you know."

"Okay."

"I'm going to try and get some sleep now."

And I'm officially fully awake.

"Okay," I said. *I didn't know what else to say.* "We'll, talk soon?" *Better.*

"Sounds good."

Ohhhh! This was too much for my brain. I didn't like it when the ball was in my court. I did like Bryce though … more than as a friend. I could no longer deny that truth. *But what now?* I heard Jade tapping on her crib. Good, a distraction. I'm sure there were all types of distractions in her diaper waiting for me too. I couldn't make the mistake of taking too long to respond to Bryce like I did before though. I'd planned to get back to him, that same day.

I invited my mom and Aunt Janet over for brunch; neither knew that I'd invited the other. Olivia would be there too and they'd behave themselves in front of her. Aunt Janet hadn't spent a lot of time with Jade, which I never thought would happen. But I understood. Mom had been at my place all the time since Jade was born, and I knew Aunt Janet had little interest in being in the same room with Mom, and vice versa. But since Mom hadn't been around as much, I hoped Aunt Janet would increase her visits. *I would love that.* But this day was about reminding these two sisters how much they needed and missed each other. When I thought about it, Mom's overbearing antics with Edna, which were a bit much even for her, were probably due in part to the absence of Aunt Janet in her life.

"Someone's at the door Bailey," said Aunt Janet from the living room.

"Would you get that for me, please?" I said from my bedroom and winked at Olivia who was in on my plan.

"Sure."

Then Olivia and I listened. The front door had been opened but we didn't hear anything after that. We looked at each other.

"What do you think is happening?" Olivia asked me.

I raised my shoulders.

"We don't go out there until we hear some laughs though," I said.

"I think you should settle for words or sounds of any type, or I may miss graduation."

She was right. Jade was out there with them in her playpen so I was confident that my baby would break that tension. After about twenty minutes of not hearing much, I decided to do something.

"Put on your shoes, Olivia. Then follow my lead."

"Okay."

We walked into the living room where Mom and Aunt Janet were on the sofa playing with Jade … together. *Nice.* They both gave me a look though. *Not nice.*

"Hey Mom," I said. "We'll be back in a few. Come on Olivia."

"Where are you going?" asked Mom.

"Errands," I said, and then we left.

Six hours later, Olivia and I returned. We'd seen a movie, gotten pedicures, had lunch, and visited a few grocery stores to look at baby food packaging for ideas. When we got back to my place, we put our ears to the door to gauge what we were about to walk into.

"Do you smell that?" asked Olivia.

I sniffed and widened my eyes. We entered the apartment and joined Mom and Aunt Janet in the kitchen cooking. *Yay!*

"Well, hello," I said. "What have we here?"

Neither of them responded but they both smiled at me. And then Mom plucked me on the head before kissing me. Then Aunt Janet gave me a hug.

"Can we have brunch again next Sunday too?" Olivia asked.

"Yeah," said Aunt Janet.

"Sure," said Mom. "But will you two be joining us next time?"

Olivia and I looked at each other and then looked at Mom and nodded.

Right before I turned in for the night, I decided to send Bryce a text message. I planned to call him but it had gotten too late, and I didn't want to wait until the following day to communicate.

My text said: "I think us not being friends is probably a good idea." And then I sent a smiley face emoticon.

He replied with a smiley face too.

A DIFFERENT KIND OF MONDAY

I had a great weekend, which is probably why I didn't flinch when I saw all of the folders on my desk. If I had given the weekend a theme it would definitely have been "Relationships: Restored & Upgraded." I needed to think of what to tell Christina during lunch when she asked about my weekend. I was not good at lying. *Ha, I know you don't believe that.* I'll just mention what I did without mentioning Bryce, for now.

A delivery guy appeared in my doorway with a bouquet of gorgeous calla lilies in a vase, which I assumed were for Carrie until I signed for them. They were from Bryce; his card said, "Ever had a wish come true? You were mine." I called him.

"Well, hello there," he said.

"I just received a gorgeous array of my favorite flowers. You are so sweet."

"I'm glad you like them."

"I do. Thank you. It was a nice surprise."

"You're very welcome."

"Were you able to sleep last night?" I asked.

"Yes, I was actually. I fell asleep with a smile on my face."

"Good. I hope I had something to do with that."

"You had everything to do with that," he said. "I wanted to ask if you'd accompany me to my law association gala next Friday."

"This Friday? How long have you known about said gala?"

"I've known for a couple of months, but I had no intention of going. But once you kissed me —"

"*I* kissed *you*?"

"Yeah. Once *you* kissed *me*, I figured we should probably go to the gala."

"Um, hmm. Apparently my *faux-nesia* is contagious."

He laughed.

"I would love to join you at your gala."

"Great," he said. "And … would you be going as my girlfriend?" *And there it was. Smile.*

"Is that what you want?"

"Very much. Yes."

"Me too."

"Perfect."

"Well, boyfriend, I'd better go. Talk to you later?"

"Definitely. Bye beautiful."

Okay, now I can tell Christina.

I *tried* to be productive after that conversation. It was tough, especially with the flowers on my desk, which I continued to stare at. And my responsibilities at knirD weren't slowing down, so I ended up delegating even more of my work to team members. That made them more competitive, with each other coveting the next big assignment from me, so I eventually delegated everything, which freed up time to work on my own venture.

Christina and I discussed when the best time would be to recruit Peter—the unappreciated snack-food genius who reported to William. If we did it too soon, and he mentioned our plans to someone, it could hurt us. If we waited too long, we'd waste time that we could've used to recruit someone external. Once Carrie retrieved all of the client data, we decided to go for it. At this point, any additional information or potential hires that we acquired would've been gravy.

A couple of days later, Christina, Peter, and I had lunch away from the office at Sirio's. Peter was sold. We went over the details of his offer, some of our preliminary business plans, and had him sign nondisclosure and confidentiality agreements. When Peter left, Christina and I discussed plans to approach Chase. We both liked him, but if he didn't come on board, we didn't want him to have any knowledge of what we were doing. She left the decision up to me and told me to trust my gut.

On my way back to work, I got a call from Carrie.

"Dennis has been asking me questions about where you are. He's never done that before."

"Hmm, okay thanks for the heads up. I need to keep my lunches to an hour going forward."

"Yeah, maybe."

"Okay, I'm on my way back."

I texted Christina about Dennis's sniffing around. She reminded me to be extra careful because Dennis had eyes everywhere. *So true.*

When I got back to work, Carrie and I congregated briefly in my office. I asked her to treat the day as if it was her last day by inconspicuously clearing out anything personal in her desk, removing anything personal from her computer, and backing up any and all data we needed. She said that she'd already done that but would do a final check.

"Should today be my last day here?" she asked.

"No, but it can be any day soon. And just in case it's not up to us when that happens, let's not leave anything behind."

"Got it."

I took that same advice. Then I gazed up at the ceiling, and remembered the day I got the office and no longer had to sit in a cubicle. I was so excited then — the new responsibilities and future potential, some came to fruition, but a lot hadn't. Then Chase was in my doorway.

"Looks like your mind was just a million miles away." Now he was standing in front of my desk.

"Something like that."

"It's good to be back in New York. I've gotta tell you, I'm so tired of traveling. I remember being told that I'd have limited travel in this role, and now it seems like I'm on a plane heading to California every week."

Should I ask him? Come on gut; tell me something. "I want to ask you something, Chase."

"Sure, shoot."

I hesitated. *I shouldn't do this here.* "Could we talk tomorrow? Maybe over lunch? I want to bounce some ideas off you." I wanted to make sure it didn't sound like a date, since many of the ladies here got red in the face every time he walked by. And I also didn't want him to know that it wasn't knirD-related.

"Sure, but how's Monday instead? I've got a ton of meetings this week."

"Works for me."

"Cool. Speaking of meetings, I have one in five minutes. Gotta run."

"See you — wait. Did you come in here for something?"

"Nope."

I worked for a few hours before calling it a day. Bryce was meeting me at my place ... again. He'd made a concerted effort to spend evenings with me and not work late. Now sometimes he'd be on his laptop, but it was a compromise that I was okay with. *I loved the time we spent together.* He played with Jade, gave Olivia advice, and let me bounce business ideas off him. He'd been in my exact shoes before and now had a very successful practice.

"So these are your final days at knirD. How do you feel?"

"I don't think I really thought about it until this week because I've been so busy. But I've reflected on the last year there and everything that has gone down. I feel ready for the next chapter. Very ready."

"That's a good feeling."

"It is. I know you can relate."

"I sure can."

"Can you believe how big she is now?" I asked holding Jade.

"I know. We'll have to start planning her first birthday in a few months." *He said "We."* Olivia came running out from the back.

"Aunt B, question. What's the name of that store you love to go to—"

"Ha!" Bryce chimed in. "She loves them *all* Olivia."

I hit his arm. "Not all of them," I said. "What's that store you got those hideous shirts from that time?" I asked him.

"Anyway," said Olivia. "I'm talking about the big one that's on Lexington Avenue?"

"Oh, Bloomingdales," I said.

"Yes! Bloomingdales. I was thinking of going there. Is it expensive?" she asked.

"No, it's not expensive to *go there*," I said, and Olivia looked relieved. "It's only expensive if you buy stuff."

"Ha!" Bryce said again.

"Ha, ha, Aunt B." Olivia made a face and headed back to her room.

"It's true," I said to Bryce.

He shook his head. "Since your mom hasn't been here, I have to ask. Is there anything in the fridge that we can turn into dinner?"

"I am offended. No mom means no groceries? Of course there are items here that can be … substituted for a dinner-*like* meal."

Bryce said, "Umm hmm. That's what I thought. Chinese, Mexican, or pizza?"

"Pizza!" Olivia yelled from her room.

"That girl hears everything," I said.

"She really does."

I stroked his face, pulled him in, and kissed him. Then Jade started patting Bryce's face hard so we took a break.

Then he said, "I love you."

I was taken aback. I didn't know if he'd really said it or something that *sounded* like it. My expression must have given away that I was figuring that out in my head.

"I love you." He said it again.

"I love you too," I said, and we were kissing. "You know," I said. "I think English is officially our second language now to kissing." He chuckled and we were back at it until Jade tried to stand on my lap.

"I'm going to approach Chase on Monday and see if he wants to join me and Christina."

"Cool. What's your plan?"

"I'm thinking an off-site conversation, over lunch."

"Okay. What are your main concerns?"

"The biggest is that he won't be interested and will then tell Dennis about my plans. I don't want anything to impact our success, especially in the beginning. Dennis would get to knirD clients and try to prevent any potential business for us."

"That's understandable. That's a gamble you might have to take, though."

"I know. The other thing is that Chase may want to be a partner instead of the head of brand management. I haven't worked with him long enough to know if I want to get in bed with him at that level."

"I don't like that analogy."

"Sorry.

"At all."

"Sorry, sweetie. I just mean that he's good, but I can't confirm that he should be co-leader of my dream. You know?"

"I know."

"As head of brand management, he'd be contributing his expertise at a high enough level, but if he ended up not working out, it's easier to ... release him than it would be a partner."

"Are there any pros to his being a partner?"

I paused for a moment then said, "No, there aren't."

"Then you need to be prepared to refute any potential proposals from him, because he may ask to be a partner."

"You're right. I need to think that part through some more," I said. "I love you."

He looked at me and said, "I love you too. And I said it first."

"You're supposed to say it first."

"Says who?"

"Says the *the Manual for Non-Desperate Women,* 2014 edition."

"Really? Women have said it to me first before."

"Exactly. Where are these women now?"

He was about to say something, then he thought against it.

"Um hmm," I said.

"So what I deduce from what you're saying—"

"Before you start deducing, just concur that I'm correct. My methods are obviously effective."

"Have you ordered the pizza yet?" asked Olivia from the other room.

"*Nooo.*" Bryce and I said in unison.

"I can't believe she's off to college in a few weeks."

"I know. Are you ready for that?"

"Of course not. That's my Olive … Maybe she can—"

"She has to go to college, Bailey."

"You don't even know what I was going to say."

"I had an idea," he said. "So this Chase … he's unattractive, right?"

"He's really tall. Like six-foot-six."

"Oh, okay."

Bryce knew about my weirdness with height. Telling him Chase's height was like telling him that Chase had teeth in his third eye.

CINDERELLA MOMENTS

I decided to work from home on Friday, so I wouldn't feel hurried getting ready for Bryce's gala. Edna would be with Jade and Olivia would be by after school to help. I had my hair done during lunchtime, so I felt relaxed by the evening.

Bryce had texted me throughout the day. *He's so cute.* I felt as though we were going to the prom. And, of course, he had time to text me; there was no hair for him to get done; no mani or pedi to keep un-smudged all day; no Spanx to maneuver into. *I'm sure he got a haircut, but he does that every week anyway. Men. They've got it so easy.*

Olivia wanted to do my makeup, so we started that early in case she had me looking like Cyndi Lauper circa 1983. That would allow me time to undo and redo. But Olivia actually did a great job. She turned me into this elegant red-carpet-worthy glamazon, and she didn't even use a lot of color. I loved it.

I had some time to kill before Bryce arrived, so of course I played with Jade until she was worn out and fell asleep. Then

I realized that I had only five minutes left to get ready … so I added twenty minutes to that and was good to go.

After the *oohs* and *ahhs* from Olivia and Edna, I looked at Bryce, and he was speechless. *Perfect.*

"Ready?" I asked.

"Um, yes. You look — beautiful. My goodness, you look amazing," he said and caressed my face. Olivia took several photos of us with her phone.

"Okay, we have to go now," I said.

"Okay, okay," Olivia said as she continued to take paparazzi-like photos of Bryce and me walking away, waving, and then exiting. He held my hand to the elevator and wore the biggest smile. It made me smile.

"I'm sorry I kept you waiting. You look very handsome, too, by the way."

"No apologies necessary. If this is the outcome it was beyond worth the wait." *He got points for that one.*

There was very little talking during the elevator ride down.

"I'm a lucky man."

"This is true. And you've ruined my makeup."

"Wait, there's still a little bit of lipstick right —" and his lips were on mine again until we heard someone clear his throat. We were at the lobby level, and there was a group of people waiting to enter the elevator.

"Oh, sorry." *He wasn't sorry.* Bryce escorted me to a limousine that was waiting outside for us.

"A limo," I said, as the chauffeur opened our door. "Very nice."

"I'm trying to impress you."

"It's working."

"It's Friday. The traffic and parking will be crazy. This way we can just relax. Plus I'd get a ticket trying to do this while driving. But in a limo—" And his lips were on mine again.

Then Bryce and I held hands for the remainder of the ride.

It was the most boring law association gala that ever took place on dry land—ever. *But* I had the time of my life. If you asked us who else attended, we couldn't tell you. We danced, ate, and drank all night long. We didn't associate with anyone; it was terrible but so perfect.

We drove around in the limo for another hour after the gala. Manhattan is cool after midnight when there's no traffic, well little traffic. I've known Bryce for about a decade—back when we all worked together—and he had always been a great and dependable friend. And now here we were, a couple.

"After all these years, finally, I get the girl."

"After all what years?"

"Never mind. Have you called all your little boyfriends to tell them that it's over? That you're with me now?"

"No, silly. I just sent them text messages."

"Ha, ha, ha." *He knew that was funny.*

We drove around some more and continued our laugh-talk-athon. After a while, I started to get tired, so we drove to my place. Then we were in front of my building, leaning against the limo and each other like teenagers.

"So is there any chance that I'll get lucky tonight?"

"Of course."

"Really?"

"Um hmm. But there's an even higher chance that you won't." I laughed; he didn't. *He knew that was funny too.* I pulled him in to change the subject until his crotch started moving. I pulled away but he held onto my hand and followed me into the building. *Damn, he's making it hard. No pun intended.*

Knowing that there was a camera in the elevator, I should have exercised more restraint, but Bryce smelled good and felt good. *Damn. Come on thirty-ninth floor!* If I had any more floors to go, Jade would have been a big sister in nine months for sure. *Ding! Okay, it's time to exit.* Bryce walked out of the elevator with me, and then I stopped him in his tracks.

"Bryce."

"Yes?"

"I'll see you tomorrow."

"It is tomorrow," he replied and pulled me in. Technically, he was right.

"Okay, then I'll see you next week."

"No, no. I'll see you tomorrow. Later today."

"Okay," I said. His face was shiny; his shirt was out of his pants and disheveled. *My bad.* I started to tuck his shirt back in his pants but immediately realized that that was a bad idea when I got poked back, so I kissed him and then I left.

As I walked down the long hallway to my apartment, everything inside me wanted to turn back. But I thought about Olivia and setting a good example. She didn't know that I had known Bryce for years. If I had walked in at noon with the same clothes on, no conversation would have undone whatever message those actions sent. And even though I'd known Bryce for a while, he hadn't been my boyfriend for even a full week yet, so I was doing the right thing. *I am, even though my body and previously dry panties totally disagreed.*

OOPS, GOOD-BYE

The following Monday morning, I stopped at the deli for a toasted cinnamon bagel with butter before heading to work. That was my routine during my first year at knirD. I'd grab a bagel, a fifty-cent coffee — in the blue and white cup — and the *New York Times*. Once I realized that carbs were against me, that I could read the *Times* online, and it was more chic to drink five-dollar lattes, my morning habits changed. But for old time's sake, I picked up a blue and white coffee and the *Times* too.

I entered the elevator and realized that my cell phone needed to be charged. It wouldn't even turn on. *Ugh. Why do I always let this happen?*

I headed toward my office. Carrie's desk was super neat. I wondered where she was. *It's after nine.* I put my key into my office door, and it didn't work. I tried it again. *The key won't turn at all. Oh my God.* I tried it one more time, but it still wouldn't work. I got an unpleasant feeling in my stomach, and then I looked around the office. I placed my coffee and bagel on Carrie's desk, put the *New York Times* under my arm, and walked. I wasn't sure where I was heading to yet, but I couldn't just stand in front of my office. *Damn, where's Carrie? What's going on?* This was the worse time for my phone to be powerless. I decided to walk toward the restroom and passed by Tori's desk. She was an admin.

"Good morning, Tori. Would you happen to have a phone charger that'll work with this?" I showed her my phone.

"Hi, Bailey. I do, actually." She dug through her desk, pulled out a charger, and handed it to me.

"You are a life saver. Thanks so much. I'll get this back to you later!" I said as I headed quickly toward the ladies room.

The ladies room was empty. The only wall outlets were near the sink, which was too public to have a conversation. I entered the larger wheelchair-accessible stall, which had a sink, mirror, and outlet. *Perfect.* I plugged in the charger and turned on my phone. I called Carrie but got her voice mail, so I hung up. Then I called Christina, but hung up and decided to text her instead in case someone walked in on the conversation.

I texted Christina: "My key didn't work in my office door, and I don't know where Carrie is."

Christina texted back: "OMG! Where are you now?"

I replied: "In the ladies room, using a borrowed phone charger."

Christina texted me back: "Give it a few minutes, and then go see if Carrie is at her desk. Don't use your limited phone juice to call her. I'll call and text her."

I replied: "Okay."

I paced the bathroom stall, impatiently waiting to hear from Carrie, assuming we'd both been fired. My phone beeped, then I ran to the sink where it was charging, but it was just a calendar reminder. *Carrie, where are you? What is happening?*

Someone came into the bathroom, so I stopped pacing. She entered a stall and began her business, which got serious. I unplugged the phone, grabbed my things and exited, so I wouldn't acquire the scent that was about to permeate the place.

I headed back toward my office, walking slowly while observing the movements and conversations of everyone. No one was really paying much attention to me, so that was a good sign. As I got closer, I saw Carrie sitting at her desk, so I picked up the pace and felt a bit of relief—especially once I got closer and saw that she was eating my bagel, sipping my coffee, and bobbing her head to whatever was streaming through her earphones. I tapped her on the shoulder, and she removed her earphones.

"Good morning, boss. Thanks for the breakfast."

I was confused—and fuming. "Good morning?" I replied in an angry whisper. "Where were you? We've been calling you. My office key doesn't work. You weren't at your desk. I thought they fired you—us."

Carrie hopped up and said, "What? It doesn't work?"

"No," I replied and dug in my handbag for the keys. She took them and tried to open the door. The door opened—very easily, actually. She turned around and looked at me. Then she tilted her head. I walked past her and into my office; she removed the key and closed the door.

"Which key did you use?" she asked and handed me my keys.

"This one. No this one."

"That's not your office key."

"Wait. What?" She was right. I was using the wrong key. I dropped my head, and she patted my back. Then she was about to say something but just ended up laughing. I had to join her. *What a start to the day.*

"I'll leave you to your work," she said, and then left, leaving the door open.

I plugged in my cell and texted Christina an update. I received a horde of LOL replies.

"Oh, sorry. My phone was on silent. I just saw the missed calls," Carrie said from her desk.

"Um hmm. By the way, that was *my* breakfast."

She ran to my doorway and said, "It was? I'm so sorry. It was delicious, though." She hardly got that last word out before she cackled again.

"Get out of my doorway." I threw a pen at her.

After I was able to calm myself down from this morning's self-inflicted ordeal, I got some real work done. Christina and I had decided on a logo from three that I'd created; we negotiated pricing with a packaging company for our first line of products, and we decided on three additional knirD employees to poach. *Yeah, by work I mean work on my business.*

Chase popped into my office and said he couldn't do lunch because of a meeting, so we postponed it. That was fine because after the morning I'd had, my *trust bucket* was shrinking, and I was having second thoughts about the conversation with Chase—that moment anyway. So, instead, I went to Christina's for lunch, and we crossed off a few more to-do items while inhaling sushi before I headed back to work. *I'd kept lunch to an hour this time, though.*

By three o'clock, we'd covertly acquired not three but four more knirD employees, including a rock star paralegal.

I cleared my desk of any trace of non-knirD related work, and it was just in time because Dennis walked into my office and sat directly across from me.

"Hey," he said.

"Hey."

"How's Christina doing?" he asked, playing with his ID badge clipped to his belt loop.

"She's fine." I didn't engage in small talk with him anymore, so I wondered where this was going.

Looking at his ID badge, he said, "I never liked my ID photo. Do you like yours?" Now he was looking at me.

"Yep. Mine is fine."

"Can I see it?" he asked. *Weird.* It was on my desk, so I handed it to him. He looked at my photo, and then he looked at me for a few seconds. "And your office keys."

We looked at each other, and then I realized what was happening. *Oh snap.* I dug in my purse and put my office keys on the table. He picked up the keys, looked at me and said, "Get out. Now."

I picked up my handbag and favorite photo of Jade. As I stood, two security guards entered my office.

"Please come with us," said one guard.

I exited the office, and they followed behind me. Carrie stared, frozen. Everyone watched as I headed toward the elevator. *I could hear my swallows in the quiet.* Chase walked to his office doorway to see what was going on, and then he saw me. We locked eyes for a minute, and he looked genuinely shocked, so I assumed he was clueless about everything.

I walked into the elevator, and the two *knirD avengers* walked in after me. We were the only ones in the elevator, and I stood behind them.

I quickly texted Christina: "It happened. I'm on my way over. Get out the champagne."

Christina replied: "OMG — Yay! OMG. And will do!"

Then I texted Bryce: "It happened."

He immediately texted me back: "You heard?"

I replied: "Huh?"

And then Bryce replied: "Elly and her husband were just arrested."

I texted Christina again: "Make that two bottles of champagne."

NEW OLD BEGINNINGS

The weekend before our new office opened, I probably slept a total of five hours, but I was so pumped about what lay before us and how things had fallen into place—if I had been tired, I didn't even know it. Edna-the-nanny needed a week off, so my parents had taken Jade to Brooklyn for that week, and I was able to focus on the business without getting sidetracked by Jade's big beautiful brown eyes.

On opening day, our team of seven started the day with a big catered breakfast, and we collectively shared our dreams and hopes for the first year. As the CEO, I ended our powwow with a speech and a prayer. Then I handed everyone a Ziploc bag.

"We won't be catering again until we're in the black, so divvy up those muffins and bacon in these bags and put your name on it."

We spent a lot of our first month conducting focus groups and sampling some of the food items we planned to roll out, and the results were so good that we had follow-up sessions to ensure the first round wasn't a fluke.

Chase reached out to me shortly after my departure from knirD, and we were supposed to meet on several occasions, but now I was the one postponing the meetings. Our team was working so well together, and I fully trusted each team member. I was a little uneasy about bringing Chase into the mix because, once he had access to all that we were doing, he could impact us negatively if he shared any of it with knirD. Christina was on the fence as well but was leaning more toward bringing him on board than I was. On the plus side, Chase had great ideas, a great network, and we could have used someone to develop and oversee the brand-management side. Christina and I were swamped with our own duties, allocating as much time as possible on brand management, while preventing complete disownment from our significant others.

By our third month, we had two successful products under our belts. We weren't generating any real revenue just yet, but we were getting enormous media exposure. We also got our products into the hands of some celebrity moms, magazine editors, and decision-makers at a few healthy grocery food chains. Christina's husband's colleague's wife was a fashion stylist for some of the news anchors and TV personalities in the city, mostly women who were mothers. So, that was how we got our products into some hands initially. From there it was word of mouth and attending dozens of events. It was just ... fun! We were both so passionate about the products, research, meeting people, and pitching ideas that being great friends only made it better.

Things were looking up. I brought Jade into the office a few hours a week with Edna-the-nanny in an effort to alleviate the guilt I felt on the days that I worked past seven o'clock, which were now down to only one a week. Aunt Janet came by often to check out my latest venture as well. She was so proud of me. Things between her and my mom were so much better. They'd congregate at my place often and took Jade out all the time.

We ultimately decided to hold off on Chase and, in the meantime, Christina found an awesome brand-management consultant who had turned out to be a godsend. It actually made the most sense for our business financially — consultants don't get stock, benefits, or paid for Thanksgiving. And I must say that working at a woman-owned company gave me immense gratification, too, especially after my last gig. Six months into our venture had been more rewarding than the decade I'd spent at knirD.

On Fridays, I took my time going into the office, especially since I usually worked late the night before. It was almost ten o'clock in the morning when I strolled into the office while trying to end a phone conversation with Mom.

"I'm okay with you taking Jade to Brooklyn today, Mom."

"Okay, the last time I took her, you were nervous, so I wanted to remind you that she's in great hands, and she can have fun *outside of Manhattan*." I may have offended Mom the last time, but it was the first time that Jade had been away from home more than a day, so I may have worried too much, verbally.

"I know, Mom. And I appreciate you taking her so that Bryce and I can have a quiet dinner at home. I really do."

"Okay, honey. We'll head out at about two o'clock to beat the traffic."

"Sounds good. I've gotta go, but I'll talk to you later, okay?"

"Okay, Bye."

I walked into the break room, and Christina was grinning from lobe to lobe.

"Hey Chris. What's up?"

"Nothing. Was that your mom?"

"Yeah, she's taking Jade to Brooklyn for the night. Bryce is cooking dinner, so we'll have the place to ourselves. It's a rare moment."

"Very nice." Christina was smiling *too* much.

"Why are you weird?"

"Nothing. It's just nice, that's all."

"You know, I kinda want to go out to dinner—"

"No! Don't … you can always go out. Let him cook dinner for you."

"I was going to say that he'd prefer a quiet night in anyway, so that's fine too." I waved my hair out of my face, and Christina took my hand.

"You've got to get a manicure. Today."

"I don't have time today. It's already after ten, and I have a ton to do." I walked toward my office, and Christina followed me.

"No, you have to. I'll book the appointment for you."

Shadé Akande

"Christina?"

"Yeah?"

"It's not a priority for today. I can do it over the weekend."

"*Nooo* ..." Then she sat down at my desk and crossed her arms.

"Spill it. What's going on?"

"Your nails are really chipped."

"I hate that more than you do. Why do you care? How'd you even notice? We have a million things to sign off on, and I've only reviewed half of them—and you want me to go and get my nails done?"

"Yes, for your dinner tonight."

"My dinner *at home,* where I'll likely be in a t-shirt? Again, why are you being weird?"

Christina started playing with her hair and avoided eye contact with me, which meant that she knew something. She was *horrible* with secrets, so this was going to be easy. I leaned against my desk next to where she was sitting and stared at her.

"Okay, okay!"

"What? Spill it."

"You have to get your nails done because they have to look nice tonight."

"Why do they have to look nice tonight?"

"Hmm?"

"Christina!"

"Because Bryce is going to propose! Because he's going to propose ... and then kill me."

My jaw dropped.

"Propose?" I asked.

"Yeah. You can't have *man-hands* with diamonds." Christina said and stood up.

"Propose?" My eyes got watery.

"Yeah." Christina took my hand, and my tears gave way. *She just said propose.* Then my mind went into plan mode, and I started pacing in my office.

"I need to get my nails and hair done. Oh! Maybe I can get my makeup done by the Christian Dior girl."

"Okay, if you look like a freakin' beauty queen when he shows up tonight, Bryce is going to know that I told you."

"What are you trying to say? What do I look like now?"

"You look like a beauty queen now. Just one who hasn't slept ... or actually won a title."

"What! Wait, do I have bags?" I rushed to my mirror. "I have bags under my eyes?"

"You do not have bags. Look—" Christina grabbed my shoulders. "Get your nails done and come back to the office to do *some* work. Then head out of here a little early to spruce yourself up—at home. No appointments or cosmetic undertakings; just a shower and some lip-gloss. Okay?"

"Okay, you're right. He'll be coming straight from work too anyway. You're right."

"Good."

Then we both sat down and were quiet.

"He's going to propose!"

"He's going to propose!" We jumped around like teenaged girls.

And then I grabbed Christina and asked, "Did you see the ring? He showed you the ring didn't he?"

"I—"

"Don't tell me! Wait ... no don't tell me."

"Okay." Christina turned to head out of my office because she knew that I would likely bug her some more. "I'll book the nail appointment for you now."

"Thanks. Carrie has the number." *I knew she had no idea where to call.*

"Okay, good."

"Oh, I saw your favorite vampire teen actor at Bryce's office the other day."

"Really! Oh my gosh—is Bryce representing him?" Christina was way too enthusiastic.

"I didn't ask, but they're working on something."

"Did you take his picture for me?"

"No."

"Why not? You're always taking pictures."

"Because he's a child, and I'm a grown woman."

"Well, how'd he look in person?"

"Like he'd get *you* seven to ten years in prison."

"Ha ha. I'm not asking for *me* ... it's for my girls."

"Umm hmm."

"It is."

"I believe you." *I didn't believe her.* Then she popped back into my office.

"Oh yeah, we said that we should find a woman with kids for the ad we're going to run. Remember?"

"Yeah, did you think of someone?"

"I did. I was talking to my neighbor yesterday and she recommended her cousin who'd do it if we partner with her charity—and it's a children's charity."

"Nice. Who's her cousin? Have we met her?"

"Gwen Stefani."

"Wha—"

"Oh, that's my phone. We'll talk." Christina left.

We're getting Gwen Stefani for our ad—via Christina? I put my head on my desk.

PRESENT DAY

I left work at about four o'clock, so that I'd have time to shower and pretty up before Bryce arrived at six o'clock.

The place is clean and quiet. The fridge is — well, Bryce is bringing groceries. I feel so much joy and peace and love and all the good stuff that fairytales lie to little girls about, but it is really happening this time.

I'm about to turn on some music, but there's a knock at my door. It's only five-thirty, but I'm glad he's early because the anxiety is killing me. I need to play it cool, though.

I check my teeth in the foyer mirror, take a deep breath, and open the door. There's a man standing there with a lot of hair on his head and face. I look at his eyes. I know those eyes.

He says, "My ID had this address on it."

I put my hand over my mouth.

It's Eric.

===